HEIRESS'S
ROYAL BABY
BOMBSHELL

HEIRESS'S ROYAL BABY BOMBSHELL

JENNIFER FAYE

MILLS & BOON

First published in Great Britain 2018
by Mills & Boon, an imprint of HarperCollins*Publishers*
1 London Bridge Street, London, SE1 9GF

Large Print edition 2019

© 2018 Harlequin Books S.A.

Special thanks and acknowledgement are given to
Jennifer Faye for her contribution to the
The Cattaneos' Christmas Miracles series.

ISBN: 978-0-263-08211-1

Printed and bound in Great Britain
by CPI Group (UK) Ltd, Croydon, CR0 4YY

PROLOGUE

Mid-August, Milan, Italy

A CASUAL PARTY full of joy and hope for the future was just what she needed.

It was her chance to forget that her opinions were unwanted and disregarded. That acknowledgment sliced deep into her heart. But she refused to become a silent shadow in her own family.

Noemi Cattaneo, heiress to the Cattaneo Jewels dynasty, welcomed the loud music and the sound of laughter. After yet another argument with her older brother, Sebastian, she needed space. She took a drink from her second glass of pink champagne. When was he ever going to treat her like an adult instead of his kid sister and realize that her opinions had merit?

She took another sip of bubbly, hoping to cool off her rising temper. Every time she recalled her brother saying that being a *silent partner* suited her, frustration bubbled within her. How dare he tell her to stick to modeling! There was more to her than her looks—a lot more. And she refused to spend the evening worrying about her brother.

Someone bumped into her. The champagne sloshed over the edge of the glass and onto Noemi's new white dress. She glanced down at the pink stain starting at her chest and streaking down to her midsection.

She might need to cool off, but this wasn't how she'd intended to do it. Noemi's gaze lifted as she looked around for the klutz who'd bumped into her, but she couldn't pinpoint the culprit. They hadn't hung around to express their regret. Maybe coming to this engagement party hadn't been such a good idea.

She searched the crowd for Stephania, her friend who'd convinced her to come to the party. As Noemi's gaze scanned the room, it strayed across a man with mysterious hazel eyes. He was standing across the room surrounded by a half dozen eager, smiling women. Even though each woman appeared to be vying for his attention, he was staring at Noemi. Her pulse quickened. This wasn't the first time that she'd noticed him staring her way.

"Hey, Noemi," Stephania said. "What are you doing standing over here all alone?"

"Apparently getting champagne spilled on me."

Stephania gasped when she saw the stain. "I'm sure they have some club soda around here."

Noemi shook her head. "I'll just go home."

"But you can't leave yet. We just got here. Besides, if you go home, you'll just mope around."

And think about how her brother refused to give her any respect. Noemi hated to admit it but Stephania was right. Her gaze strayed to the tall sexy stranger. His eyes caught and held hers. Her pulse quickened. Perhaps there was a reason to stay.

Twenty or so minutes later, with the help of club soda, paper towels and a hair dryer, Noemi's dress was once again presentable. By then, she'd talked some sense into herself about the attractive man whose gaze seemed to follow her around the room. He was probably the type who enjoyed the chase—not the capture.

However, there was something slightly familiar about him. Not one to keep up with gossip or who to know, Noemi couldn't place him. But if he was at this exclusive gathering, he must be someone important.

She glanced around the room but didn't see any sign of him. Disappointment assailed her. This wasn't like her. She could take guys or leave them. She thought of asking Stephania if she knew the man's name but shrugged off the idea. Her life had enough complications. She didn't need more.

But just the same, her mood had dimmed. Her problems once again started to crowd in around the edges of her mind. Needing some fresh air, she stepped out onto the terrace. There was just enough of the evening sun for her to admire the distant mountain range as a gentle breeze caressed her skin.

"Beautiful."

The deep rich voice had her turning her head. And there stood the intriguing stranger with the mesmerizing eyes. His voice held a slight accent. She couldn't place it, but it was extremely sexy—just like the rest of him.

"I'm sorry. Am I disturbing you?" She glanced around for his harem of women, but he appeared to at last be alone—with her.

"Not at all. Please join me." He motioned for her to join him at the edge of the terrace.

She stepped closer but not quite the whole way. "You were admiring the mountains, too?"

He sent her a puzzled look.

"When I stepped out here, you said beautiful. I assumed you were referring to the view."

He smiled and shook his head. "No. I was talking about you. You are beautiful."

She'd been complimented many times over the years. Being the face of Cattaneo Jewels, compliments came with the job. But the man looked at her as though he wanted to take her in his very capable arms and devour her with hungry kisses. The heat of a blush engulfed her cheeks.

"Thank you."

The warm August evening was no help in cooling her down. She knew it was polite to make small conversation, but for once, her mind was a blank. This man didn't seem to know who she was, and for the moment, she found that to be a welcome relief. She didn't want him to treat her differently. For tonight, she wanted to be just a face in the crowd.

But when she turned her head and gazed into this man's eyes, her heart began to race. For a moment, she glanced at his mouth. If she were someone else tonight, would it be wrong to give in to her desires—to live in the moment?

But then she realized if she wanted people to take her seriously, she couldn't give in to her whims. No matter how delicious they may be.

"We should probably get back inside before people start to wonder where we've gone," she said, though there wasn't any part of her that wanted to return to the party. She was quite content to stay right here with him.

He leaned in close. "Let them wonder. I like it much better out here, especially now that you are here."

She cocked her head to the side and looked at him. "I'm starting to understand."

His brows drew together. "Understand?"

"Yes. I understand why all the women surround you. If you flatter them like this, they simply can't help themselves."

The worry lines on his face smoothed and a devastatingly sexy smile lifted his lips. "Trust me. I have done nothing to encourage those women. But when it comes to you, it's different. What brings you to such an exclusive party alone?"

She wanted to believe him when he said she was different. His words were like a soothing balm on her bruised ego. Her parents and her brother might think she should remain nothing more than a silent partner, but this man wanted to hear what she had to say. A smile lifted her lips.

"I'm not alone." The smile immediately

slipped from his face. Then realizing how her response must have sounded, she was quick to supply, "I came here with a friend."

"And your friend doesn't mind that you're out here instead of inside with them celebrating the engagement?"

Noemi couldn't help but notice his strange wording. "Do you even know the engaged couple?"

"As a matter of fact, I don't."

Noemi's mouth gaped. Only the very famous or the very rich who knew the couple had been invited. The newly engaged couple didn't want the paparazzi to know the details. They wanted a chance to celebrate and enjoy the moment. And he was a party crasher.

She tilted her chin upward, taking in the man's handsome face. He didn't strike her as the type to intrude upon a stranger's good time. His chiseled jawline gave his face a distinctive look. But it was his mesmerizing eyes that held her gaze captive. The breath caught in her throat.

And then the urge once again came over her to kiss this stranger. But she didn't even know him. She glanced away. She was letting his good looks and sexy smile get to her.

Maybe if she got to know him a little better.

There was something about him that made her curious to know more about him. "So if you don't know the engaged couple, why are you here?"

He shrugged. "The host of the party invited me."

She took in the man's straight nose and fresh-shaven jaw. "Do you live in Milan?"

He shook his head. "I'm just passing through."

"On your way to where?"

He shrugged. "I haven't decided yet."

The fact he didn't live in Milan—that he was moving on—appealed to her. The last thing she wanted at this juncture in her life was a relationship. She had her modeling career to focus on—even though it was rapidly losing its appeal.

But an evening of fun—an evening with no strings—what would be the harm? Tomorrow she could decide if she wanted to continue to fight for a more significant place in the family business or look elsewhere. Just then, the French doors burst open and a couple wrapped in each other's arms stumbled onto the veranda. When they bumped into Mr. Tall and Sexy, they straightened up.

"Sorry about that," Matteo DeLuca, an award-winning actor, said. "We didn't know anyone was out here."

The young woman in his arms burst out in a giggle. Her eyes were glazed and as Matteo led her away, she tripped over her own feet. Upon their exit, they forgot to close the doors. The loud music and cacophony of voices came spilling forth.

Noemi's companion closed the doors and then turned back to her. "How would you feel about going someplace quieter?"

"But I don't even know your name."

His brows rose ever so briefly. She couldn't help wondering if his reaction was due to the fact that he expected her to know him. Or whether he was surprised that she'd resisted jumping at his offer. Because right at that moment, she couldn't think of anything she'd like better than spending the evening with this intriguing man.

She took a moment to study him. His dark designer suit definitely didn't come off a rack. As he took a drink of what appeared to be bourbon, she noticed his watch. A Rolex no less. This man looked right at home at this party.

He smiled and his eyes lit up. This man, he was... Well, he was confident. It was in the way he stood with his broad shoulders pulled back and his chin held high. But he wasn't un-approachable either. He seemed to have a sense of humor. But most of all, he came across as the type to go after what he wanted. And right now, he appeared to want her.

"My name is Max."

"Max, huh?" She tried the name on for size. It wasn't as imposing as Zeus or Hercules but it'd do—it'd do just fine.

"You don't like my name?"

"It's not that." It's that it was such a simple name for such a complicated man. And yes, she sensed there were many facets to this man in the ten or so minutes that they'd been talking.

"Then what is it?"

She shrugged. "I just wasn't expecting such a common name."

He smiled and it made her stomach shiver with nerves. "I won't tell my mother you said that."

"Please don't." They were acting like one day soon she would meet the woman. That was never going to happen. But it was fun to play along with him.

"And what's yours?" His voice interrupted her troubled thoughts.

"My what?"

Amusement twinkled in his eyes. "Your name?"

"Oh." Heat rushed up from her chest and settled in her cheeks. "It's Noemi."

"Noemi. That's a beautiful name for a very beautiful woman." He took a step closer to her, leaving little distance between them. She searched his face for any sign of recognition of who she was. There was nothing in his expression to suggest that he recognized her as an heiress to the infamous Cattaneo Jewels worn by the rich and famous worldwide. But there was something else reflected in his eyes.

Desire.

Their gazes locked. This gorgeous hunk of a man, who could have his pick of the eligible women and some not quite so eligible at this party, desired her. Her heart raced. It'd been such a long time since a man had turned her head. But there was something special about Max.

The *thump thump* of her heart was so loud that she could barely hear her own thoughts. And then he reached out to her. His thumb ever so gently traced down her jaw before his finger brushed over her bottom lip. It was such a simple gesture but it sent a bolt of heat ricocheting from her mouth down to her very core.

Before she could figure out how to react to these unexpected sensations, his gaze lowered to her lips. He was going to kiss her?

Her heart lodged in her throat. She should... She should do something. But her body betrayed her. Her feet refused to move and her chin lifted ever so slightly.

As though that was all the invitation he needed, Max lowered his head. Her eyes fluttered closed. She shouldn't want this—want him. But she did, more than she thought possible.

His lips were smooth and warm. And a kiss had never felt so good. She didn't make a habit of going around kissing strangers, but in the short time she'd spent with Max, she had this uncanny feeling that she could trust him.

She slipped her arms up over his muscled shoulders. As the kiss deepened, her hands wrapped around the back of his neck. She'd never been kissed quite so intently and with such unrestrained passion. She wasn't even sure her feet were still on the ground.

Suddenly Max pulled back. It happened so quickly she had to wonder if she'd imagined it. But her lips still tingled where his mouth had touched hers. And he sent her a dazzling smile that promised more of the same.

If she were wise, she would end things right here, but her body hummed with unquenched desire. For once, she wanted to throw caution to the wind and enjoy herself. After all, her brother accused her of being impulsive. Why not live up to the accusation…just this once?

Max pulled his cell phone from his jacket pocket.

"What are you doing?" The words slipped from her lips.

"I'm calling my driver." And then he spoke into his phone. Seconds later, the conversation ended. He turned back to her. "The car will be waiting for us downstairs in a couple of minutes. Shall we?"

But she'd never said she would go anywhere with him. Was it that obvious in the way she looked at him? More than likely he was taking his cues from that kiss they'd shared. That short but arousing kiss.

"What are you thinking?" His eyes searched hers.

"I was thinking…um…that it would be nice to go somewhere a little quieter."

He smiled again. "My thoughts exactly."

He held his arm out to her. It took her a moment to figure out what he was doing. Did men even do that anymore? Wasn't it just something she saw in the old black-and-white movies that her mother collected?

But Noemi found the gentlemanly gesture endearing, even if it was a little dated. There was something about this man that was so different from anyone she'd ever known and that appealed to her. She had a feeling this evening was going to be totally unforgettable.

CHAPTER ONE

Three months later
Mont Coeur ski resort, the Swiss Alps

WHAT WAS SHE going to do?

Noemi paced back and forth in her luxurious bedroom in her family's palatial chalet. A gentle fire flickered in the fireplace, keeping her suite cozy. She couldn't sit still.

So much had happened in the last few months that it made her head spin. First, the pregnancy test had turned up positive. As she'd struggled to come to terms with what this meant to her future, she'd stumbled across the fact that she had a long-lost brother. The realization had jarred her entire world. How could her parents have kept Leo a secret all her life?

An ensuing row between her and her parents had her shouting out hurtful words—words she didn't mean. And yet now she couldn't take them back. She couldn't tell her parents she was sorry and that she loved them.

They were dead.

The reading of their will had succeeded in driving home the fact that her parents wouldn't be here at the chalet as was their Christmas tradition. But the three siblings intended to spend the holiday together.

It had been strange to meet her brother Leo for the first time, even stranger to hear the contents of her parents' will. She never would have imagined that the terms of the will would be the way they were. Clearly Sebastian hadn't either, because when he'd discovered that his parents had given Leo controlling shares in Cattaneo Jewels for six months, he'd been furious. And although Leo had been clearly reluctant, the terms stated that should Leo refuse, Cattaneo Jewels would cease trading and be liquidated. And none of them had wanted that.

But tempers and emotions had risen, and it was all Noemi had been able to do to convince her brothers to think on it and to return here to the chalet in Mont Coeur just before Christmas for the final decision.

Even now, she could only guess at what her parents had been thinking when they'd written the will and its unusual terms. She missed them dearly—most especially her mother. She needed her now more than ever.

Noemi swiped at her eyes as she thought of her mother. And though their last conversation had been heated and hurtful, Noemi didn't doubt her parents had loved her—even if she had made mistakes along the way. But all the wishing in the world wasn't going to erase the last angry words that they'd exchanged, nor would it bring them back to her.

Noemi moved to the French doors in her room and stared out at the cloudy afternoon sky as big lazy snowflakes drifted ever so slowly to the ground. It was a light snow. The kind that melted as soon as it touched the roads. And any other time she'd be caught up in the peaceful relaxing view. But not today.

She was running out of time to keep her secret to herself. Her hand pressed to her slightly rounded abdomen. No amount of baggy clothes was going to hide her pregnancy much longer.

And what was she supposed to say to people when they asked who the father was? *His name is Max? He has the dreamiest eyes that appear to change colors to suit his mood? And his body is like a sculpture of defined muscles? Or when he laughs it is deep and rich?* Even now, his memory brought a smile to her face.

After the most magical night, he'd insisted that it would be best not to exchange full names or phone numbers. She'd hesitantly agreed. Neither of them had been looking for a lasting relationship. And now that she really needed to speak to him, she didn't know how to reach him. She'd even asked Stephania about him, but she didn't know him—

Noemi's cell phone buzzed. She moved to the bed and picked it up. She wasn't in the mood to speak to anyone, but when she saw that it was Maria, her sister-in-law and close friend, she answered.

"How are you doing?" Maria asked.

"Okay. I guess." Noemi sighed.

"Really? I'd hate to hear you if something was wrong."

"What's that supposed to mean?"

"You're usually bubbly but lately you've been really down. Is it your parents?"

"No. I mean, I miss them a lot."

"So something else is bothering you?"

Maria had always been good at reading her. And she was the closest thing Noemi had to a big sister. If she didn't talk to someone soon, she was going to burst.

Noemi worried her bottom lip. "Can I tell you something?"

"Sure. You know you can always talk to me. Is it about the reading of your parents' will?"

Noemi shook her head and then realized Maria couldn't see her. "It's not that. But if I tell you this, you have to promise not to say a word to Sebastian."

There was a slight pause on the other end of the phone.

"Never mind," Noemi said. "I never should have asked you to keep anything from my brother."

"It's okay. You need someone to confide in and I promise your brother won't hear a thing from me. Sometimes he can be a bit overprotective where you're concerned."

"And when he hears about this, he's going to hit the roof. He'll be just like Papa—" She stopped, recalling how poorly her parents had taken the news of her pregnancy.

Even though her parents had had a child in their teens and had given him up for adoption, they'd still been disappointed with her unplanned pregnancy. What was up with that? It wasn't like she'd set out to wreck her life. She'd thought that out of all the people in the world, they would have been the ones to understand. They hadn't. And it had hurt Noemi deeply. Worse yet, they'd died before she could ever put things to right.

"Relax." Maria's voice drew Noemi out of

her thoughts. "We'll figure out how to deal with him."

"Thanks. But I'll deal with him."

"Whatever you want. But you still haven't told me your problem. Maybe I can help. Perhaps it isn't as big as you're imagining."

"No. It's bigger." Noemi's insides quivered with nerves. By saying the words out loud, it was going to make this pregnancy real. Just like the reading of the will had made her parents' deaths startling real. Once she told Maria about the baby, there would be no more pretending. In less than six months, she was going to give birth.

"Noemi..."

"I'm pregnant."

Silence. Utter and complete silence.

Noemi's heart raced. Her hands grew clammy. And her stomach churned. What was Maria thinking? Was she disappointed in her, too, just like her parents had been?

"Are you sure?"

Noemi nodded. "I took three home pregnancy tests and then I went to see the doctor. It's official."

"I don't know what to say." There was a pause as though Maria was searching for the right words. "How do you feel about it?"

"I knew I wanted kids someday, but not yet—not now. I'm only twenty-six."

"And the father, how does he feel?"

"I… I don't know."

"Noemi, you've told him, haven't you?"

She inhaled a deep breath, trying to calm her nauseous stomach. And then she launched into how she'd met Max and how stupid she'd been that night. She'd been hurting and not thinking straight. And she thought it would be a good time without any strings.

"Don't worry. Everything will be all right," Maria said, though her voice said otherwise.

"Even you don't believe it. What am I going to do? I'm not going to be able to hide my condition much longer. Most of my clothes don't fit."

"I know." Maria's voice rose as though she'd just discovered the answer to all Noemi's problems.

"What?" She was desperate for some good advice.

"You need some retail therapy."

Noemi's shoulders drooped. That was the very last thing she wanted to do. "Are you serious?"

"Yes. I'm very serious. What are you doing right now?"

"Maria…"

"Tell me what you're doing?"

"Pacing in my room."

"And that is helping you how?"

"I'm thinking."

"And so far it hasn't gotten you any answers. You need to get out of that chalet. The fresh air will do you good. Shopping is just what you need."

"Is that what you did when you and Sebastian separated?" And then realizing that she was touching on a very painful subject, she said, "Forget I said that. I'm just not myself today."

"Actually, it is what I did."

"Did it help?"

"Temporarily." Her voice filled with emotion. "Enough about me. I hope you know that if I could manage it, I'd be there with you, but trust me, after you buy some Christmas presents and new clothes for yourself that are comfortable, you'll feel much better. There's nothing worse than squeezing into clothes that don't fit."

Maria had given birth to Noemi's nephew, Frankie, nearly two years ago. She knew a lot more about pregnancy than Noemi. Maybe she was right. She glanced over at her discarded jeans on the bed. She'd barely gotten them buttoned, but she hadn't been able to pull up the zipper. And no matter how much she enjoyed her leggings, she couldn't stay in them forever.

"You'll do it, won't you?" Maria prompted.

"Yes, I'll go."

"Good. Call me later and let me know how it goes."

After the conversation ended, Noemi still wasn't certain that shopping was the right thing to do, but what else did she have to do considering she was at the chalet alone? Her gaze moved to the discarded jeans on her king-size bed. No way was she going to put those on again. Her black leggings would have to do.

She moved to the walk-in closet, hoping she could find something to wear besides her T-shirt. She sifted through the hangers until she strayed across a white long-sleeve V-neck knit tunic. It was loose but not too baggy and it'd go great with her leggings as well as her knee-high black boots.

With her wardrobe sorted, she was ready to head into the village. She would search for some roomier clothes and see what she could find for Christmas, which was only a few weeks away.

He didn't want to be here.

Not really.

Crown Prince Maximilian Steiner-Wolf, known to his friends as Max, sat in the back seat of his sports utility vehicle as one of his three bodyguards maneuvered it along the windy road in the Swiss Alps. His bodyguard and friend, Roc, sat in the passenger seat while Shaun, a bodyguard of similar stature and looks, sat next to him. He couldn't go anywhere without at least a small security detail.

Being the crown prince came with certain nonnegotiable restrictions. One of them was his safety. He may insist on traveling but the king demanded that his safety always be taken into consideration. It was a hassle but the guards were very good at becoming invisible unless their presence was required.

Max turned his head to the window and stared out at the snowy landscape of the mountainous region with some of the best slopes in all Europe. He was planning to spend a week or two skiing at Mont Coeur before returning to the palace in the European principality of Ostania.

He hadn't been home in months, but the approaching holidays were a big thing, not only at the palace but also throughout Ostania. And his mother had called, insisting he spend Christmas with them. After all, he was still the crown prince, even though he would never be king. However, the royal family was still keeping up appearances with the public.

Though Max was the firstborn and had been groomed from birth to take the throne of the small European country, no one had foreseen that he would be diagnosed with cancer in his teens. Although his treatment had been successful, doctors informed him that the cure had very likely rendered him sterile. Royal decree stated that the ruler of Ostania must produce an heir verified by a paternity test. From then on, Max knew it was impossible for him to take the throne.

So as not to cause the nation to panic over the future of Ostania, the palace had kept Max's infertility quiet while attentions turned to preparing his younger brother, Tobias, to become the future ruler of Ostania. No one outside of the court circle knew, and meanwhile, to the world, Max was still the crown prince.

While all of his parents' attention was showered on his little brother, Max roamed the world. He wasn't as much of a party animal as the press claimed him to be, but he did know how to have a good time. However, that was all about to change.

The truth was he was tiring of his partying

ways. Moving from city to city, beach to beach and resort to resort was growing old or maybe he was getting old. In the beginning, it had been fun. The freedom had been intoxicating, but now he was starting to get a hangover from too much partying. He needed to do more with his life and to do that he had to go home—he had to officially step down from his position as crown prince in order to find his future.

That acknowledgment stabbed deep into his heart. He'd always been competitive. His parents had raised him that way. And stepping aside to let his younger brother take his place didn't come naturally to him. But it was more than that—it was knowing he was letting down his family—his country.

His stopover in Mont Coeur was to be his last. After he hit the slopes and cleared his head, he planned to return to Ostania to have a difficult talk with the king and queen. It had been put off long enough. Then he would lead a quieter, more productive life.

The SUV slowed as they entered the heart of the resort. Max instructed the driver to pull to a stop outside a ski supply shop. He'd lost his sunglases at the end of last season and he needed a new pair of shades before hitting the slopes.

Not waiting for his security to get the door for him, he let himself out. He'd just stepped into the narrow road when someone with a camera pointed at him. Max inwardly groaned. It was going to be one of those trips where he was besieged for photos and autographs. Normally it didn't bother him, but right now he had a lot on his mind.

"It's the Prince of Ostania!" someone shouted.

Everyone on the sidewalk turned in his direction.

Quickly his security guards flanked him. None spoke. They didn't have to. The serious look on their faces said they meant business. Being recognized didn't happen all the time. However, it happened more than Max would like.

Security escorted him around the vehicle. He forced a smile as he passed the tourists and then dashed into the shop. He hoped the people wouldn't follow him.

Inside the shop, the walls were lined with snowboards and skies. In the background, "Let It Snow" played. Colorful twinkle lights were draped around the checkout where the workers wore red Santa hats with white pom-poms on the tips.

Figuring it might be easier to search for the

sunglasses on his own, he bypassed the people at the checkout who were openly staring. He turned into the first aisle and nearly collided with a pretty young woman. She flashed him a big toothy smile. He intentionally didn't smile, not wanting to encourage her attention. He gave a brief nod and excused himself as he made his way around her.

Ever since he'd met Noemi, no other women had turned his head—not the way she had. And yet, he'd let her get away without even getting her number. He'd thought at the time that he would get over her quickly. That's the way it'd been with the other women who'd passed through his life. But there was something different about Noemi.

She acted tough, but inside where she didn't want anyone to see, there was a vulnerability to her. She'd let him get close enough to gain a glimpse of her tender side. Much too soon, she'd hidden behind a big smile and a teasing comment.

He could clearly recall her beautiful face. Her brown eyes had gold specks like jewels. And when he closed his eyes, he could feel the gentle touch of her lips pressed to his. With a mental shake, he chased those thoughts to the back of his mind.

It didn't take him long to find what he wanted and then he strode to the checkout where the pretty woman was standing, pretending to check out a display of lip balm while she stared at him.

He pretended not to notice as he paid the clerk. All he wanted now was to get to his private chalet and unwind. However, when he pushed open the front door and stepped onto the sidewalk, the crowd had multiplied. Flash after flash went off in his face.

CHAPTER TWO

MAYBE SHOPPING HADN'T been such a bad idea.

Noemi clutched the colorful shopping bags stuffed full of goodies and headed for the door. She'd purchased some jeans in a bigger size that had spandex in them, making them so much comfier. They fit her a lot like her leggings. She'd pulled on the waistband and was surprised by how roomy they were without being baggy.

She'd also found some loose blouses and sweaters that hung down to her hips. For a while, they would hide her growing baby bump. It wasn't the figure-flattering clothes she normally wore, but it was so much better than what she had before. And she just wasn't ready for maternity—not yet.

As Maria had suggested, Noemi had taken time to do some Christmas shopping, including purchasing two designer sweaters. One for her newfound brother, Leo, and one for Sebastian.

She and Sebastian might disagree—heatedly at times—but she still loved him.

With big black sunglasses and a gray knit beanie pulled low, she stepped outside the store and started up the sidewalk toward her car. The snow clouds had passed and the sun shone once more. Up ahead a crowd of people swarmed the sidewalk and spilled out into the roadway. She glanced around, wondering what was going on.

She would love to turn and avoid the crowd, but they were standing between her and her vehicle. And her numerous bags weren't light. She kept moving toward them. Surely the crowd would part and let her through.

She was on the edge of the group when an excited buzz rushed through the crowd. Noemi paused and turned to a young woman who was holding up her cell phone as though to snap a picture.

"Do you know what all the fuss is about?" Noemi asked.

The young woman with dark hair pulled back in a ponytail smiled brightly. "It's the best thing. Crown Prince Maximilian Steiner-Wolf has just arrived."

Noemi had heard the name before, but she knew nothing of the man. It seemed as though she was in the minority as the crowd continued to grow.

Noemi glanced around, curious to see the prince.

The young woman pointed to the shop in front of them. "He's in that store. Right there. Can you believe it? But his bodyguards aren't letting people in."

Noemi felt sorry for the guy. As the face of Cattaneo Jewels, she'd had her fair share of exposure to publicity, but the crowd of people forming around the store was extreme even to her. "And everyone is just standing around waiting for him to come out?"

The young woman gave her a look like she'd just grown a second head. "Well, yeah. Of course."

Noemi nodded in understanding, even though she didn't. Her arms ached from the weight of the bags. She continued to make her way to her car.

"Excuse me," Noemi called out, finding it difficult to thread her way through the crowd.

A cheer rose in the crowd. Then the crowd rushed forward. At last, there was room to walk.

Thud!

Someone ploughed right into Noemi. She

lurched forward. In an effort to keep herself upright, she lost her grip on the packages. They fell to the ground in a heap. Her arms waved to the side as she tried to steady herself. Suddenly there were strong hands reaching out, gripping her by the waist.

Once she'd regained her balance, she turned and found herself staring into intriguing hazel eyes. It was Max. Her heart lodged in her throat. What was he doing here? Waiting to see the prince?

"Noemi?" His eyes widened with surprise. And then a smile lifted his lips. "I'm sorry. I didn't see you."

He bent over and started to pick up all her bags. She hadn't realized until then just how many packages there were, but Christmas was her favorite holiday. She had to make sure she bought something for everyone. Maybe more than one thing for everyone—especially her young nephew. It was going to be a difficult Christmas without her parents. And she felt driven to do everything possible to make the holiday bearable.

But right now, her thoughts centered around the father of her baby. And here she'd been thinking she would never see him again. She averted her gaze from him as she knelt down next to him. She scrambled to gather her packages.

"What are you doing here?" she asked.

He scooped up most of the packages and straightened. "I was planning to go skiing."

When she straightened, she had to lift her chin in order to look him in the eyes. And that was a dangerous thing to do because every time she gazed into his eyes, she forgot what she was about to say.

Just then a flash went off. And then another. And another.

"What's going on?" She glanced around as everyone was looking at them. And then the lightbulb went on in her mind. "You." Her gaze met his again. "You are the prince?"

His jaw flexed as his body stiffened. "Yes. I am Prince Maximilian Steiner-Wolf."

Her mouth gaped. Realizing that everyone was watching them, she forced her mouth closed. How was this possible? Was she really that out of touch with reality that she'd missed the father of her baby was royalty?

She had so many questions for him, but they lodged in her throat. This wasn't the time or the place to rehash the not-so-distant past.

"Come with me," he said.

Not waiting for an answer, he took her hand and led her to a waiting black SUV. With the help of two men, they reached the vehicle without people stepping in their way.

She wasn't sure it was wise being alone with him, not when he still filled her dreams, but it beat being in public where everyone was watching them and eavesdropping. Once inside, she turned to him. She needed answers. She needed to know why he'd kept his title from her. She needed to know so much.

"Not now," he said as though reading her mind. Turning to the driver, he said, "Go."

"My vehicle is back there," Noemi said.

"Don't worry. We'll come back for it. Later."

The driver, as though used to driving through crowds, safely maneuvered the SUV past the sprawling mass of people.

She turned to the window and stared blindly at the passing shops. This had to be some sort of dream. Perhaps she'd fallen back there and hit her head. Yes, she thought, grasping at straws. She'd hit her head and this was all a dream. Because there was no way that she was pregnant with a prince's baby.

"Noemi?" Max's voice cut through her thoughts.

She had absolutely no idea what he was asking her. She turned to him. "What?"

"I asked where you are staying."

"Um…" She thought about returning to her vehicle and decided that Max was right. Later would be better to pick it up. "Take a left at the next intersection."

His dark brows rose. "Those are private residences."

She nodded. Her neighbors were some of the most prominent actors and actresses, athletes and notable figures in the world. Since she'd been coming here all her life, she took it all for granted. But now, seeing it from a stranger's perspective, she realized that it might be impressive. But to a prince? Nah.

He was probably wondering why she lived in such an exclusive neighborhood. Apparently she wasn't the only one in the dark. He didn't recognize her even though her face had been plastered on every glamour magazine as well as television promos for a number of years.

She gave the driver directions to her family's chalet. When they reached the gate to the exclusive community, she put her window down and assured the guard that it was okay to let them through.

"I've never been to this part of Mont Coeur,"

Max said. "I've always preferred to have my accommodations close to the slopes."

As they passed the large and impressive chalets, she noticed that most displayed Christmas decorations. Some sported a door wreath while others had a bit more. Normally their chalet was the most festive of them all—but not this year. Her father had always taken care of the outside decorations. However, this year Noemi had done it by herself and the twinkling lights weren't quite as spectacular as prior years.

Her palms grew damp as her heart raced. She couldn't relax, not with Max next to her. She didn't know what made her more nervous—the fact that they'd spent the night together or the fact that the man she'd slept with was royalty. When Maria heard this, she was never going to believe it.

He longed to kiss her berry red lips.

The memory of their sweetness taunted him.

Max gave himself a mental jerk. Now that he'd found Noemi again, the last thing he wanted to do was scare her off. What were the chances of them running into each other again?

Slim.

Had she figured out his true identity and

planned this reunion? Not possible. He hadn't decided on coming to Mont Coeur until last night. Even then, he'd only told his trusted staff.

Max gazed over at Noemi. Her posture was stiff and she kept her face turned away. He wondered if the source of her discomfort was from their collision, the run-in with the fans, learning he was a prince or all of the above.

Normally learning that he was the crown prince had women falling all over him. But Noemi had pulled away. In fact, if she sat any closer to her door, she'd fall out. Most interesting. He'd thought they'd both enjoyed their time together.

But it wasn't too late. He still had a chance to find out if there was truly a spark between them.

When the SUV pulled to a stop in front of a luxurious chalet, Noemi said a quick thank-you followed by goodbye. It'd be so easy to just let her go. He'd still have his good memories, but he'd never know what had been real and what had been part of his wishful imagination.

As he watched her head for the front steps, he told his security team to wait for him. He hopped out into the snowy driveway and followed her.

"Noemi, wait."

For a moment, he didn't think she was going to stop. Her hand reached for the doorknob, but then she hesitated. She turned to him but didn't say anything. Her gaze didn't quite meet his. She stood there waiting for him to have his say.

"You didn't even tell me your last name. I don't want to make the same mistake twice." When she sent him a puzzled look, he added, "Letting you get away without knowing your name."

"Oh. It's Noemi Cattaneo."

"Your name. It sounds familiar."

"You've probably heard of our family business. Cattaneo Jewels."

Of course, he'd heard of them. Who hadn't?

"Your family's business has the distinction of handling some of the world's finest and rarest jewels."

"Have you done business with us?"

"Not me personally, but my family has." He was getting off point. "Anyway, I wanted to say…" his Adam's apple bobbed "…I'm sorry. I've handled this all wrong."

"It's not your fault that people recognized you."

"No." He shook his head. "Not that. I'm sorry for before, when I insisted that we keep things casual and not exchange phone numbers." He stepped closer to her. "I've been thinking of you—"

"Don't." She shook her head. "I don't need your pity."

"It's not pity. I—I just handled things poorly before. And I want to apologize."

Her gaze momentarily widened but then she glanced away. "We did the right thing. Our lives are too diverse. I mean you...you have a country to run. And I am... I mean, I have things to do."

He'd never witnessed Noemi nervous before, not that they'd spent a lot of time together. But in the time he'd known her, she'd come across as confident and fun. The Noemi standing before him was different and he wanted to know what had changed her. Why did she avoid looking at him directly?

He is a prince?
How is that possible?
Noemi had so many conflicting emotions flooding her body that she didn't know what

to say to him. Part of her longed to fall into his arms and pick up where they'd left off before. But logic told her to tread carefully. Max was a very powerful man. There was no way she was going to blurt out that she was pregnant with his baby. Finding out that he was royalty changed everything. She needed time to think.

"Have dinner with me?" His voice stirred her from her thoughts.

She shook her head. "I don't think that's a good idea."

The hopeful look on his face faded. "Was our time together that forgettable?"

"It definitely wasn't forgettable." The words were out her mouth before she realized she was revealing too much. She'd barely been able to think of anything else these past few weeks since learning she was pregnant.

That wasn't exactly true. She'd thought a lot about him ever since they parted—even before she'd learned she was pregnant. She would wonder what he was doing and who he was doing it with. And she wondered if he ever stopped to think about her.

"That's good to hear," he said. "So we'll do dinner."

She recalled the mass of people waiting for him outside the ski shop. She couldn't even imagine the spectacle they'd make by having dinner in public. It would be an utter zoo.

Though it pained her to say, she uttered, "We can't."

"Sure we can." He smiled like he had all the answers to their problems.

Again, she shook her head. "Everyone knows you're here at the resort. They'll all be on the lookout for you."

"And you don't want to be photographed with a prince?"

She glanced away and shrugged. The ramifications of the photo would be catastrophic once her pregnancy became known. Until she had a plan for this baby, she didn't want to make any more mistakes, especially where the public was concerned.

He laughed. "Do you know how refreshing you are?"

He was amused? Her lips pressed together into a firm line. She didn't know what there was to be smiling about, but then again, he didn't know about the baby.

She lifted her chin. "I don't care to be laughed at."

"I'm not laughing at you." His amusement faded. "I think you're amazing." As though her lack of response went unnoticed, he said,

"Most women I've met would fall over themselves to have dinner with me. But not you. Which makes me that much more determined to see you again. In fact, I'm not leaving here until you agree to have dinner—no strings attached."

"Not tonight." She wanted to clear her head—and do an internet search.

He arched a dark brow. "I have the feeling if I let you get away tonight that there won't be another chance for us to get together. You'll always have an excuse. And I can't stay here forever—no matter how tempting that may be."

"I promise we'll do it another time."

"Must I beg, *ma chérie*?"

"You speak French?"

He nodded. "French and Italian as well as English. Ostania is situated near France, Italy and Switzerland. We speak French but it's heavily influenced by the surrounding countries. I could tell you more about my country over dinner."

It wasn't his country that she was interested in learning more about. And they did have much to discuss. Her hand instinctively moved in the direction of her tiny baby bump, but she caught herself in time and lowered her arm to her side.

"If you're worried about privacy, we can have dinner at my condo." A hopeful look reflected in his eyes.

"You're serious, aren't you?"

He nodded. "I've never been more serious in my life."

She didn't miss the part of a wealthy, devastatingly handsome prince begging her to have dinner with him. But as much as she wanted to spend more time with him, there was another part of her that worried about what would happen when he learned of the baby. Would he reject her? Would he reject his own flesh and blood? Or would he try to take the baby from her? The thought of it sent a chill through her.

Proceed with caution.

The only way she would find the answer to any of these questions was if she were to do as he asked and dine with him. Not sure if it was the right decision or not, she said, "Okay. I'll have dinner with you."

He didn't hesitate. "I'll send a car for you at seven."

She shook her head. "I can drive." And then she recalled that she'd left her car back in the village. "Except my car is still in the village."

"I'll send my car. And if you give me your

keys, I'll make sure your car is picked up and waiting for you at my condo."

That would be convenient, but it would also make her an easy target for the paparazzi. And she wasn't ready to be a headline on every gossip site.

She checked the time on her phone. "You may send your car for me at…seven fifteen." That should give her just enough time to sort through her purchases to find something appropriate to wear and do an internet search. "Does that work for you?"

Both his brows rose. She wasn't sure if he was surprised that she hadn't fallen all over herself to do as he wanted. If that's what he expected of her, he was in for a surprise. With a baby on the way, she had to stand firm and speak up when necessary.

Max gave a curt nod. "I'll see you then." He turned for his vehicle. A few steps later, he paused and turned back. "Is there anything specific you would like for dinner? Perhaps something you've been craving?"

Craving? Did he know about her pregnancy? She sucked in her stomach. As he continued to stare at her with an expectant look on his face with no hint of suspicion, she realized he'd meant nothing by his choice of word.

She shook her head. "Anything is fine. I'm not a picky eater."

That response rewarded her with another surprised look on his face. Apparently the prince wasn't used to women who weren't picky. She wondered just what sort of women he normally dated, but she resisted the urge to ask.

"I'll pick something special." He turned and walked away.

The desire to run in the house and head straight to her computer was overwhelming, but she restrained herself. She waited until he was inside his vehicle before she let herself in the chalet. With the door shut, her movements became rushed. She threw off her hat and coat before kicking off her snowy boots. And then she took the steps two at a time.

She grabbed her laptop from the desk and threw herself down on the bed. Her fingertips moved rapidly over the keyboard. Maybe it wasn't right snooping on the internet, but now that she knew her baby's daddy was a famous royal, she had to learn more. From her own dealings with the paparazzi, she knew most of the articles would be fiction or wildly exaggerated. But that didn't stop her from looking—

Noemi's breath caught in her throat as she

caught sight of headlines splashed across the screen that were worse than she'd allowed herself to imagine. In fact, with photos to back up the headlines, she wondered if she'd been wrong about Max.

"Twin Blonde Bombshells for the Prince!"

"Prince Maximilian with Woman Number Five in as Many Evenings!"

"The Playboy Prince Strikes Again!"

"Prince Max and His Harem!"

Disheartened, Noemi closed her laptop. She'd thought the night their baby was conceived that they'd shared something special. She never imagined that she was just one more notch on his bedpost. The thought hurt—a lot.

She placed her hand upon her midsection. "What have I gotten us into?"

CHAPTER THREE

MAYBE HE SHOULDN'T have pushed. After all, he wasn't a man to beg for a woman's company—until now. What was it about Noemi that had him acting out of character? Was it her dazzling smile? Her bewitching eyes? Or her sweet, sweet kiss?

As Max sat at the desk in his bedroom suite, he gave himself a mental shake and tried to concentrate on the plethora of emails awaiting his attention. He checked the clock for what must be the hundredth time. It still wasn't even close to when Noemi was due to arrive. He sighed.

He may not be at the palace, but that didn't mean his responsibilities ceased to exist. In fact, he was beginning to think his parents gave him more than his fair share of work to make sure he didn't stray too far from the business of governing Ostania.

He still had two hundred and seventy-nine unopened emails. He groaned. How was that possible? He'd checked his email last night because he knew he'd be traveling most of today. He'd had it semi under control, but not any longer.

He wished his email was like other people's and full of spam that he could readily dismiss. However, his email was directed through the palace, where it went through stringent screenings. That meant all two hundred and seventy-nine emails would need to be dealt with personally or would require forwarding to someone else with directions.

He worked his way through the emails in chronological order. And then his gaze strayed across an email from his mother—the queen. She didn't email him often as she was a bit exasperated with him. She thought he should be at the palace acting the part of proper crown prince. She had no idea how hard it was for him to act his part because the royal court knew that when the time came, he would not be crowned king.

That role would go to his younger brother, Tobias, who at this moment was being meticulously groomed to step up and assume Max's birthright. He didn't blame his brother. If anything, he felt indebted to Tobias. His brother was the one sacrificing his youthful adventures in order to learn the rules of governing and the etiquette for dealing with foreign dignitaries.

And yet his brother had stepped up to do what was expected of him without complaint. Max would do no less. He checked the time once again and found that he still had close to an hour and a half before Noemi showed up. It was plenty of time to work through some of these emails.

He opened the email from his mother. He didn't know what he expected, but it wasn't the very cold businesslike email telling him the schedule of Christmas events and how he was expected to take on a prominent role in the festivities. He hated pretending to the whole nation that he was something he wasn't—the heir to the throne.

He closed his mother's email without responding because there wasn't anything for him to respond to. There hadn't been one personal word in the whole email. In fact, he would have thought that his mother's personal secretary had written and sent the email except for the fact it had come from his mother's private email that not even her secretary could access.

So the cold, impersonal email from his mother indicated that she thought he'd been gone too long. Or worse yet, she'd been reading the paparazzi headlines—which he might add were wildly exaggerated or utter works of fiction.

He opened an email from his own secretary, Enzo, who stayed on top of everything for him. It sorted his duties into priorities, escalating and FYI items. The only problem was the priorities were now taking up more room than the other two categories. It was definitely time to go home.

Max typed up his response to his secretary, letting the man know how to handle things until he returned to Ostania. And then he moved on to the next official email...

Knock. Knock.

Max granted access just as he pressed Send on another response and deleted the original email.

"Sir, Miss Cattaneo has arrived."

"She has?" How could that be? He'd just checked the time, hadn't he? His gaze moved to the clock at the bottom of the laptop monitor. A lot of time had passed totally unnoticed. "Please offer her a drink and tell her I'll be right there."

He closed his laptop and moved to the adjoining bathroom. He'd meant to clean up before her arrival. He jumped in the shower, not even waiting for the water to warm up.

Five minutes later, with his hair still damp, Max strode into the living room. Noemi was still there. He breathed a sigh of relief.

"I'm sorry about that. Time got away from me." He smiled at her. "Do you need more to drink?" He gestured to her empty glass on the coffee table.

"Actually, yes. That would be nice."

He moved forward and accepted her glass. "What were you drinking?"

"Water."

Water? He didn't know why that struck him as strange. Perhaps he'd become accustomed to serving wine on a date. This was just one more example of how Noemi was different from the other women who'd passed through his life.

He quickly poured water from a glass pitcher. "Here you go."

When he handed over the now full glass, their fingers brushed and, in that moment, he recalled the silkiness of her skin, the warmth of her touch and the heat of her kiss. With a mental jerk, he brought his thoughts back to the present.

His mouth grew dry and he decided to pour

himself some cold water. He took a drink and then sat on the couch opposite hers.

He smiled. "It's really good to see you again. I just never expected to run into you here."

She arched a fine brow. "Why? Is skiing only for men these days?"

He inwardly groaned. She just wasn't going to give him an inch. She was angry about the way they'd left things. And that was his fault.

"Noemi, about our time in Milan, I handled things poorly. Is there any chance you will forgive me? And perhaps we can start over?"

"I told you I'm fine." Her lips said one thing but her eyes said something quite different.

"The frostiness in this room is making me think I should go get my ski jacket and gloves."

Her beautiful brown eyes momentarily widened. "It's not that bad."

"Maybe not on your side of the room, but standing over here, it's downright nippy."

A little smile pulled at her lips. It wasn't much but it was something.

"That's better," he said.

She tilted her head to the side. "Why?"

"Why what?"

"Why are you trying so hard when you could have any women you want?" Her gaze searched his as if she could read the truth in his eyes.

"I've thought a lot about you since that night. I've wondered what it might have been like if we'd have had more time together."

"Really?" There was a tone of doubt in her voice.

"Do you find that so hard to believe?"

Her eyes narrowed. "It's the way you wanted it—no strings attached."

"As I recall, you agreed." He wasn't going to take all the blame for the circumstances of their parting.

The frown lines on her face smoothed. "You're right."

At last, they seemed to be getting somewhere. Perhaps they could build on this and get back to where they'd once been—happy and comfortable with each other.

He took another drink of water and then set the glass aside. His gaze rose and caught hers. "Noemi, is it possible for us to start over?"

A noticeable silence filled the room. He knew it was too much to hope that they'd recapture the magic of that special night, but he had to try. With each passing second, his hopes declined.

"Yes, we can try."

Her words caught him off guard—that seemed to be a common occurrence where

Noemi was concerned. He would need to tread carefully around her in the future.

"Would you like to eat?" he asked.

Her eyes lit up. "I would."

"Good. I hope you like the menu."

He stepped into the kitchen to let the cook know. Then he escorted Noemi to a table that had been set next to the wall of windows where the twinkling lights of the resort illuminated ski slopes trailing down the mountainside beneath the night sky.

He'd had the cook prepare something basic because he had absolutely no idea what Noemi liked to eat, other than pizza. That's what they'd had in Milan when neither of them felt like dressing and going out for a proper dinner. Since then he'd never been able to eat pizza without thinking of her.

And so, after a Caesar salad, they were served a heaping plate of pasta with Bolognese sauce topped with grated Parmigiano-Reggiano. He didn't have to ask if Noemi approved of it. He tried not to smile as she made quick work of the pasta. It was a quiet dinner as he didn't push conversation, wanting to give Noemi a chance to relax.

When they finished, he noticed there was

still a small pile of pasta on her plate. "I take it you had enough."

She patted her stomach. Then just as quickly she removed her hand and a rosy hue came over her cheeks. To say she was beautiful normally was an understatement, but she was even more of a knockout with the rush of color lighting up her face.

"It was amazing. Thank you." She got to her feet. "It was good seeing you again. But I should be going."

He couldn't let her go. Not yet. "Stay. We haven't even had dessert."

"Dessert? I don't have any room left. Not after that delicious meal."

"Come join me." He moved to the couch in front of the fireplace with a fire gently crackling within it. When she didn't make a move to follow him, he said, "Please, give me a chance to explain—about the way we left things."

A spark of interest reflected in her eyes. She moved to the couch. When they sat down, she left a large space between them. He hoped by the time they finished talking that the space would shrink considerably.

"The night we met," he said, "I was captivated by your beauty."

A small smile played on her lips. A good sign. Still, she remained quiet as though giving him room to explain where things had gone wrong.

"The thing was I wasn't looking to meet someone—certainly no one like you. You were like a warm spring breeze on an icy cold night. And the next morning, I received bad news from home."

He hadn't wanted to burden Noemi with the news of his father's collapse. It wasn't like they were in a committed relationship. It had been his burden to carry on his own.

Perhaps he had that in common with his father. Because when his mother had called to tell him of this father's declining health, Max had made plans to fly home immediately. He had been at the airport when his father called and told him that his mother had overreacted.

His father had insisted he was fine and told Max in no uncertain terms that he would not be welcome at the palace for a pity visit. His father had been so animated on the phone that Max had been inclined to think his mother had gone a little overboard with worry. But that didn't mean his father's lifelong battle with diabetes wasn't taking its toll on him.

Instead of flying home, his father rerouted Max to Spain. It was a diplomatic mission to encourage increased trade between their countries—something Ostania needed.

"Listen, you don't have to explain," Noemi said quickly. "You didn't mean for it to be more than a fling. And that's fine." But the tone in her voice said that it wasn't fine with her.

In that moment, he decided to tell her the whole truth. She deserved that much. "It was about my father. He was ill and my mother was very concerned about his health."

Noemi studied him for a moment. "That's why you were so different in the morning? It was the worry about your father and not regret over spending the night together?"

"Maybe it was a bit of both." When the look of hope faded from her face, he rushed on to say, "I regretted rushing things. I lost my head that night."

She arched a brow. "Do you mean that? You're not saying all this nice stuff just because you don't want to hurt my feelings?"

He shook his head. "I didn't handle the news well. My mother—well, she can be a bit dramatic when it suits her purposes—she made it sound like my father wouldn't last through the day."

Noemi moved to his side. Her gaze met his. "I'm sorry. How is he?"

Within her eyes, he saw caring and understanding. He cleared his throat. "Much better. And quite stubborn."

"I'm glad to hear that—about him feeling better. But why couldn't you have told me? I would have understood you having to leave immediately."

"I didn't want you to know. I didn't want anyone to know. Telling someone would have made the whole situation real and at the time, I wasn't ready to deal with it."

"And now?"

"Now, I regret how I reacted. I shouldn't have dismissed what we had so readily. I would have liked if we'd been able to keep in contact." He continued to stare at her, wondering if she felt the same way about him.

"That would have been nice." Softly she added, "I thought of contacting you, too."

At last, he could breathe easier. She was slowly letting her guard down with him. He could finally see a glimmer of that amazing woman who'd caught his attention from across the room at the party. He was glad he hadn't given up. He knew if he kept trying that he'd find her.

He resisted the urge to reach out and touch her. He couldn't rush things. He didn't want to scare her off. "I'm going to be here at the resort for the next week before returning to Ostania. I'd like it if we could spend some more time together."

Noemi looked as though she was going to agree, but what came out of her lips was quite different. "I don't think that's a good idea, especially with the press watching your every move."

"I'll take care of the paparazzi. They won't bother us."

"But how?"

"Trust me. I have a lot of experience evading them. So are we good?"

She shook her head. "It's more than that."

He'd come too far to let it fall apart now. "Speak to me. Whatever it is, I'll fix it."

"You can't." She stood and walked to the wall of windows.

He followed her as though drawn in by her magnetic force. He stopped just behind her. Again, he resisted the urge to reach out to her. "Noemi, I know we haven't know each other long, but I'd like to think you look upon me as a friend—someone you can lean on."

She turned to him. "I do—think of you as a friend."

"Then tell me what's bothering you. Surely it can't be as bad as the worry reflected on your face."

"No. It's worse." Her gaze lowered to the floor. "I'm pregnant."

He surely hadn't heard her correctly. "You're what?"

"Pregnant with your baby."

The words knocked the air from his lungs.

He never thought anyone would say those words to him. And now he couldn't believe it was true. At the same time, he wanted it to be real. Torn by conflicting emotions, his body stiffened. What was she hoping to accomplish with such a wildly improbable claim?

CHAPTER FOUR

SHE SHOULDN'T HAVE just blurted it out.

And now that it was out there, she couldn't take it back.

This was not how Noemi had envisioned telling Max about the baby. The truth was she hadn't figured out how to tell him this life-changing news. It certainly wasn't something you blurted out, like she'd done. The fact she was pregnant was still something she was trying to cope with. By the paleness of Max's face, he'd been completely caught off guard.

"No." He adamantly shook his head. Then his eyes narrowed on her. "It's a lie."

She refused to squirm under his intense stare. Her mouth pressed into a firm line as she started to count to ten. Her mother had taught her to do this after Noemi had shot her mouth off one too many times in school. Noemi had imagined a lot of reactions but being called a liar hadn't been one.

She made it to the number six when she

straightened her shoulders and lifted her chin. "I am not a liar. I'm pregnant and you're the father—"

"Impossible." His voice was adamant as he started to pace.

"Actually, it's quite possible. You're going to be a father in about six or so months."

He stopped and his disbelieving gaze met hers. "Have you gone to a doctor?"

"I have. It has been verified by an official pregnancy test." She could see that he was still in denial. Perhaps she should give him some idea of the changes this pregnancy had brought to her life. "I've started to grow out of my clothes. And I have morning sickness. The doctor says I should start to feel better in my second trimester."

Max shook his head again. "It must be someone else's—"

"It's not." How dare he? What did he think of her? That she got around so much that she wouldn't be able to name the father? "This baby is yours. It doesn't matter how many times you claim it isn't, it won't change the facts."

"You're mistaken."

She crossed her arms and glared at him. "You might be a prince and all, but that doesn't give you the right to talk to me this way. This pregnancy is nothing either of us planned, but now that it's happening, we've both got to figure out how to deal with it."

He stepped closer to her. There was torment in his eyes. "You aren't listening me. I'm not this baby's father. It's an impossibility."

What was he saying? He wasn't making any sense. She hadn't expected him to take this news well, but this was far worse than she'd been imagining.

She forced her voice to remain calm. "I don't know how many ways I can say this to get you to believe that you and I are having a baby."

He turned his back to her. "You need to go. Now."

"You're dismissing me?"

"Yes, I am."

Her hands clenched at her sides. Her lips pursed as she struggled to control her emotions. "Fine."

Her face warmed as anger pumped through her veins. Did he think it had been easy for her to come here? She quickly gathered her things. Did he really think she would make something like this up?

She strode to the door with her chin lifted. She refused to slink off into the night. She paused at the door and glanced back. Max's back was still turned her way and his posture was rigid.

She tried to think of something to say—some parting shot—but her pride kept her from speaking. And so without a word, she let herself out the door.

Once she was outside, tears of frustration and anger rushed to her eyes, blurring her vision. She blinked them away. She refused to cry over such a stubborn, infuriating man.

She had to be lying.

That was the only possible answer.

Max sent his staff away that evening—even his security. It may have taken a raised voice and an empty threat or two to clear the condo, but he'd succeeded. He needed to be alone.

One hour faded into another as he sat alone in the dark. Noemi's words played on his insecurities and inadequacies—things he'd thought he'd put behind him. He'd only deluded himself into thinking that he'd made peace with losing his rightful place as heir to the throne and the knowledge that he would never be able to father a family of his own. Noemi couldn't have wounded him more if she'd been trying.

Sleep eluded him that night. By the next afternoon, he'd made a decision. Without giving himself a chance to talk himself out of it, he drove to Noemi's chalet and knocked on the door.

When Noemi opened the door, he didn't give her a chance to speak. "Are you ready to admit it?"

She frowned at him. "I already admitted that I'm pregnant. I don't know what else you expect me to say."

He needed to hear her say that she'd made up the whole thing about her pregnancy. He searched her eyes for the truth. He was pretty good at reading people. And he saw nothing but honesty reflected in them. Either she'd talked herself into believing her lies…or she was telling him the truth. But that wasn't possible. Right?

He raked his fingers through his hair. Maybe he needed to come at this from a different angle.

He exhaled an unsteady breath. "Can we talk?"

For a moment, she didn't move nor did she say a word, as though weighing her options.

He couldn't walk away until he made her understand what she was claiming was absolutely impossible. "Please," he said. "It won't take long and it's important. I've been up all night thinking about what you told me."

He was beginning to think she'd refuse to let him inside when she suddenly swung the door wide open and stepped aside. "Hurry before someone sees you."

He ventured inside. After slipping off his snow-covered boots and coat, he moved toward the great room. Not sure what to do with himself, he stood in front of the darkened fireplace beside the large Christmas tree.

Noemi perched on the edge of the couch. "I know this is hard for you to believe. It was for me, too."

He turned to her. "It's not hard. It's impossible."

"Why do you keep saying that?"

He ran a hand over his unshaven jaw. The stubble felt like sandpaper over his palm. He'd come here to settle this once and for all. He couldn't stop now.

"Come sit down." She patted the cushion next to her.

He joined her on the couch, leaning his head back against the cushion, and closed his eyes. "Some of what I'm going to tell you, no one outside my family and trusted members of the court know." He opened his eyes and gazed at her. "Can I trust you?"

"I won't tell anyone."

"You already know that I'm a prince, but you might not know that I am the firstborn—the crown prince. Ever since I took my first breath, I've been groomed to take the throne of Ostania. It is a small country, but it is prosperous. However, when I was thirteen, I was diagnosed with Hodgkin's lymphoma."

Noemi let out a soft gasp.

He cleared his throat. "At that moment, my entire world stopped. Everything became about my health. I never knew it was possible to become so sick of being sick. Of course, this was all kept hush-hush. With me being the crown prince, it was decided that it was best that the citizens of Ostania not know about my cancer diagnosis."

Sympathy reflected in her eyes. "That must have been scary for you to go through."

The cancer had been more than scary, it had changed the way he looked at himself. From the time he was little, he'd known exactly who he was, what was expected of him and what his future would entail. The cancer robbed him of that identity.

After the cancer, he'd gone out into the world searching for himself—searching for a new identity. He'd done crazy daredevil stuff, from parachuting to cliff diving to bungee jumping to more responsible endeavors, such as being a diplomatic liaison for his country. Through it all, it still felt as though something was missing from his life.

"I was young. At the beginning, I was certain I could survive anything. And it helped that everyone around me was so positive. But the more aggressive treatments left me extremely sick and my positivity faltered. At one point, I gave up. I didn't think I would live to see my next birthday."

She reached out, placing her hand in his. "I can't even imagine."

"I didn't tell you that to gain your sympathy. I wanted you to realize the intensity of my treatments. I was told it was quite likely I'd never be able to father any children."

He stopped there. He didn't tell her that royal decree stated the ruler of Ostania must produce an heir. That wasn't her problem.

Nor was it her problem that after his treatments were over and the doctors had declared him in remission that the nightmare hadn't ended. The doctors had said he was likely sterile. The palace attentions had turned to preparing his younger brother, Tobias, to become the future ruler of Ostania. Max had to take a step back as his brother replaced him.

"Well, obviously they were wrong." Noemi sent him a wavering smile. "Because I am pregnant and you are most definitely the father."

He wanted to believe her. But he knew the doctors had been the best in their field. They hadn't told Max and his parents their dire warning lightly. If he was the father, it was truly a miracle. But he didn't believe in miracles.

"I just don't think this can be true," he said. "The doctors said—"

"Stop. I'm telling you it's true."

He stared deeply into her eyes. He wanted so desperately to believe her. But he was hesitant. "I need time."

"I understand."

"We'll talk again." He got to his feet and left. He needed to walk. He needed to think. He needed space.

The stakes were so high. If Noemi was telling the truth, then he would be eligible to inherit the throne of Ostania. He'd be able to assume his birthright. At last, he'd once again feel whole.

The breath hitched in his throat. He hadn't allowed himself to consider it for years. This would change his entire life—his brother's life—if it was true.

CHAPTER FIVE

A RESTLESS NIGHT left Noemi yawning the next morning.

Her first thought was of Max. By the time he'd left, he'd at least been willing to consider that the baby was his. She knew it was going to take time for him to come to terms with the news, especially after being convinced he could never father children.

After a round of morning sickness had passed, she showered. Dressed in the new clothes she'd bought while out shopping the other day, she felt much more comfortable and more confident. Whatever happened next, she could deal with it. After all, she was going to become a mother. Dealing with the unknown came with the job.

Knock. Knock.

Who in the world could that be?

She checked the time, finding it wasn't even eight o'clock in the morning. Perhaps it was Sebastian. But that didn't make sense. He wouldn't knock as he had his own key. Maybe it was Leo. They hadn't had a chance to make him a key. Maybe he'd returned early for the holidays.

Noemi liked the thought of seeing her new big brother again. She'd immediately hit it off with Leo. She rushed to the door and swung it open to find a disheveled Max standing with his hair astray, dark shadows under his eyes and heavy stubble trailing down his jaw.

"Max?"

"I've done nothing but think about what you told me. And I'd like to talk some more."

A gust of wind rushed past him and swept past her, sending a wave of goose bumps down her arms. "Come in."

When he didn't move, she reached out and grabbed his black leather jacket. She gave him a yank toward her. Once he was inside, she swung the big wooden door shut against the gusty wind. She glanced out the window to see if he'd been followed by the paparazzi.

"What are you looking for?"

Max's voice came from much closer than she'd been expecting. When she turned, she almost bumped into him. She tried to put some space between them but her back pressed against the door. She swallowed hard. Being so close to him made her heart palpitate.

"I… I was checking to see if you were followed." She sidestepped around him and moved across the foyer. From that distance, she could at last take a full breath.

"You don't have to worry," he said. "No one followed me."

"How can you be so sure? What if they saw you come here yesterday?"

"After I was spotted in the village, I activated my backup plan."

"Backup plan? What's that?"

"One of my bodyguards is a body double from a distance. The morning after the paparazzi spotted me, he departed Mont Coeur and flew back to Ostania. I and my remaining staff have since switched vehicles and residences."

Noemi arched a fine brow. "Has anyone ever told you that you're devious?"

"I don't know. Is that good? Or bad?"

"In this case, it's a good thing. And here I figured you for the cautious type."

"Cautious, huh? I did pursue you at the party. I don't think anyone would classify that night as cautious."

She turned her head to the side, but not soon

enough. She knew he saw the smile pulling at her lips. "We aren't discussing that night."

"We aren't?"

She shook her head. "No, we aren't." They had a lot more pressing matters to discuss—matters that had apparently kept him awake most of the night. Perhaps the shock was starting to wear off and reality was taking hold.

His bloodshot eyes met hers. "I shouldn't have bothered you so early. I just didn't know who else to talk to."

"It's fine. I didn't sleep well last night so I was up early." She held out her hands for his jacket. "Let me hang that up for you."

After his jacket and boots had been tended to, she led him into the spacious living room. She started a fire while he quietly took a seat on the couch. For a man who wanted to talk, he certainly wasn't saying much.

She left a respectable space between them when she sat on the couch. Even in his disheveled appearance, she couldn't deny that he was devastatingly handsome. And when he lifted his head and stared at her with that lost look in his eyes, her heart dipped.

"How can you look so calm?" he asked.

She shrugged. "I've had time to adjust to the news."

"If we hadn't run into each other, were you ever going to tell me?" His gaze searched hers.

"I wanted to, but remember, I didn't have your last name or your cell number. I didn't have any idea how to reach you."

He rubbed the back of his neck. "That's my fault."

"But it all worked out. It was as if fate made sure our paths would cross again." She paused as her stomach took a nauseous lurch.

Please not in front of Max. Her mouth grew moist and she swallowed, willing herself not to get sick—again.

"What's wrong?" A look of concern came over his face.

Great. So much for hiding it. "It's nothing."

He studied her. "It sure looks like something. You're pale. Is it the baby?"

"In a way." Her stomach lurched again. "I'll be back."

She dashed from the room, leaving Max to come to his own conclusions. She didn't have time to explain.

Was it something he'd said?

He wouldn't know. He'd never been around a pregnant woman. Sure, his mother had been pregnant with his younger brother but Max had only been a kid back then.

Max paced around the living room. Was this really happening? Was he really going to be a father? And if so, how would his family take it?

For years now, Tobias had been learning to be Ostania's new ruler. How would he feel when Max pushed him aside to resume his birthright? Would Tobias be disappointed? Or would he be thankful to have his life back again?

Max honestly didn't know how this news would impact his brother. The truth was that ever since Max's illness and the attention had started shining on his brother, they'd grown apart.

"Sorry about that." Noemi's voice interrupted his thoughts.

He glanced at her. She was still pale, but there was perhaps a bit more color in her face. "Are you feeling better?"

She nodded. "It's just morning sickness. The doctor and books say that it is common and nothing to worry about."

He couldn't see how being sick could be nothing to worry about. "Which way to the kitchen?"

She pointed toward the back of the chalet. "Why?"

"Stay here. I'll be back." He headed for the door off to the side of the large fireplace.

The kitchen was spacious. He glanced at all the white cabinets. Maybe he should have asked a few more questions—like where to find things. But it couldn't be that hard to locate what he needed.

He moved to the cabinet closest to him. He yanked open the doors. He knew what he was looking for and if it wasn't here, he'd go to the store in the village—even if it meant dealing with the crowd of onlookers.

Cabinet after cabinet, he searched. Three quarters of the way through, he opened a door and found exactly what he was searching for— peppermint tea. He set to work filling a kettle and placing it on the stove to heat up.

While it warmed, he searched a little more and located a box of crackers. He placed a few on a plate and turned to set it on the island when he noticed Noemi sitting on a kitchen stool staring at him.

"How long have you been there?" he asked.

"A while."

"You don't trust me?"

"It wasn't a matter of trust but rather curiosity." She eyed the crackers and the now boiling kettle. "Are you hungry?"

"This isn't for me."

"Oh. Well, thank you. But I don't usually drink tea."

"I think you'll like this tea. It should help settle your stomach."

The teakettle whistled. Max set to work steeping the tea. Once everything was ready, he turned to Noemi. "Why don't we take this to the living room where you'll be more comfortable?"

In silence, she led the way and he followed with a loaded tray. He glanced around at the spacious chalet, something he hadn't taken time to do the day before. Nothing had been skimped on in its construction. It had some of the finest details.

"This is a really big place for one person," he said, trying to keep the conversation going.

"It's not mine. It belongs to my parents— well, our family."

"Are your parents here?" He glanced around.

Here he was spilling his guts to her and he didn't even think to ask if they were alone. He wondered how her parents felt about the pregnancy. And then he wondered if Noemi had told them.

"No one is here." Noemi's face once again grew pale as she sat down on the couch.

"What's bothering you?" He sat next to her. "Is it my mention of your parents? If you want me to talk to them—"

"You can't." Her gaze lowered. "They, um…" Her voice grew faint. "They died."

He hadn't seen that coming. "You mean, since we met?"

She nodded as her eyes shimmered with unshed tears. In that moment, he didn't think about right or wrong, he just acted. He moved next to her, wrapped his arm around her and drew her head to his shoulder.

He leaned his cheek against the top of her head. "I can't even begin to tell you how sorry I am."

He didn't know how long they sat there with their bodies leaning on each other. His hand smoothed down over her silky hair. And when he pressed a kiss to the top of her head, he inhaled the berry fragrance of her shampoo.

When she finally pulled back, she swiped at her cheeks. "I'm sorry. I'm not normally so emotional."

"It's okay. You don't have to explain. In fact, you don't have to talk about it." He'd do or say anything to get her to stop crying because he was not good with tears. They left him uncomfortable and not sure what to say.

"Thank you for your shoulder."

"Anytime." He just hoped the next time would come with happier circumstances. "Do you have siblings?" After the words were out, he wondered if it was a safe subject.

She nodded. "An older brother—actually make that two older brothers."

That was an unusual thing to get wrong. He had a feeling there was a story there, but he was pretty certain he'd delved far enough into her life for one day.

For a moment, they sat quietly while Noemi sipped the tea and nibbled on a cracker. Then she turned on the television, letting a morning talk show fill in the awkward silence.

A half hour later during the break in a morning news show, Max asked, "Are you feeling better now?"

"I am. Thank you. How did you know about the tea and crackers?"

He glanced away. "This is what they gave me after my cancer treatments."

"And it worked?"

"Sometimes. If it didn't work, nothing did. I just had to wait it out." He looked at her, noticing the color was already coming back to her face. "Is there anything I can do for you?"

She shook her head.

"Does this just happen in the morning?"

She nodded. "I read that some women get it at any time of the day." Noemi visibly shuddered. "Sounds absolutely horrid."

"Maybe I should go now. I really shouldn't have bothered you so early."

"It's fine. I'm sure you have a lot of questions."

"I really just have one."

She leveled her shoulders and met his stare straight on. "What is it?"

"I wanted to know if you had plans for tomorrow."

Where had that come from? He hadn't come here intending to ask her out, but he could see the benefits. Getting her out of the house, doing something together might smooth out some of the tension coursing between them.

She didn't say anything at first but then she shook her head. "I don't."

"Would you like to do something with me?"

"Are you sure? You probably have other more important things that require your attention."

"There's nothing more important than us getting to know each other better," he said, meaning every word. He couldn't think about anything but Noemi and the baby.

"You don't have to do that—"

"I know. But I want to."

Her eyes flared with surprise.

In the end, they made plans for the following morning to go snow tubing. It was short run meant for kids and adults alike. But right now, he needed to get some work done and then he'd get some much-needed sleep.

"What do you mean, she's pregnant?"

"Shh…" That evening, Max gripped the phone tighter. "I don't need anyone overhearing you."

He was speaking to Enzo, his private secretary and his confidant. He had to tell someone. He couldn't keep this huge—this amazing news to himself. He was going to be a father. His world was about to change.

Enzo's normally monotone voice took on a higher pitch. "But you can't have children—the doctors said—"

"I know what they said, that the possibility was very unlikely. Not impossible."

"Your Royal Highness, do not get your hopes up. This woman is not the first to lie in order to become included in the royal family. Remember—"

"I remember." He'd tried to forget Abree. She'd portrayed herself as everything he could ever want. They'd been happy for three months and then she'd claimed to be pregnant.

When the paternity test was done, he was not the father. The extent of her lies had been devastating for him. But in the process, he'd learned she wasn't the woman she'd portrayed to him. She was nothing like he thought. Thankfully his family never found out how deep her lies had gone.

It was why he'd insisted on keeping his relationships casual since then. Until Noemi. She was different. She didn't seem to care what he thought or what he expected. She did what she wanted. And so far, she wanted nothing from him. There's no way she was lying to him. Right?

Enzo's voice sliced through Max's thoughts. "What is this woman's name? I'll run a background check on her."

Enzo didn't say it, but Max could hear the wheels in the man's mind spin. He wanted to see if Noemi was a liar, a cheat, a scam. He wanted to find every little thing she'd done wrong in her life and prove to Max that she was unsuitable for him. Because Enzo, like his parents, had very definite ideas of how a royal should act and exactly who they should marry.

"I'm not telling you," Max said with finality.

"But, Your Highness—"

"Leave it alone, Enzo."

There was a distinct pause. "Yes, sir."

In time, Max would learn everything he needed to know about Noemi, but it would all come from her. He didn't need a private investigator or a credit report. He was going with his gut on this one. And his gut said he could trust her.

To help alleviate Enzo's worry, Max said, "I will take care of the situation."

"Did you tell her about the necessity for a paternity test?"

Max resisted the urge to sigh. "Not yet."

"What are you waiting for?"

Max didn't say anything. The truth was he didn't know why he was hesitating. He hadn't hesitated when it came to Abree. He'd known from the start that she was lying. He'd insisted on the test as soon as it was safe for the mother and baby.

"Your Highness?"

"I wish you'd just call me Max." He'd never been one for royal protocol. That was his mother's thing—not his.

"That is not possible. You are the crown prince. As such, you deserve the respect due your station."

"And we grew up together. You know me. We played polo together."

"That was a long time ago, sir. And I know that when you don't want to talk about something, you change the subject."

"Don't worry. I'll take care of this."

He didn't want to. He didn't want to do anything to ruin his time with Noemi, but Enzo had a point. He couldn't stand to be played again. And his family deserved to know that their lives were about to be disrupted, once again. This time, though, the disruption would be a good one.

He would talk to Noemi in the morning about the test. Surely she'd understand. Right?

CHAPTER SIX

THE NEXT MORNING, Max decided they should talk first and play in the snow later. The stakes were high and he had to make sure Noemi understood how high.

"Max, what's wrong?" The smile had slipped from Noemi's face. "If you have to cancel our plans, it's okay. I understand."

He shook his head. "It's not that." Max leaned forward, resting his elbows on his knees. "We need to talk."

"I thought that's what we were doing."

"I'm serious, Noemi."

She sighed. "I know."

"We need to talk about the baby and the future."

"If you're about to tell me that you don't want anything to do with the baby, I can deal with it."

"What? No. That isn't what I was going to say."

She gave him a weak smile. "That's good."

"Our child will know me." Max stated it with conviction.

"Okay. Was there something else you wanted to discuss?"

He cleared his throat. "My country dictates that we must provide proof of the baby's legitimacy."

She moved back. "What are you saying?"

Surely she would want her child to be legitimate. Wouldn't she? He'd never imagined that she wouldn't want her child to be a part of the royal family—to be heir to the throne.

"You must have a paternity test done as soon as possible."

"I got that part but why?"

"So we may become a family and the baby will be heir to the throne."

She shook her head. "No."

"What do you mean no?" He got to his feet. Now she was being totally unreasonable. His child had a right—a duty to assume the throne of Ostania.

She got to her feet, straightened her shoulders and lifted her chin until their eyes met. "I know with being a prince and all that you aren't used to hearing the word no, but I'm saying it now and to you. No."

In that moment, his heart sank. He wasn't

sure if it was the thought of losing the prospect of being a father and all it entailed, or if it was the realization that once again he'd been lied to by a woman. And not any small lie—but one that was so close to his heart.

It took him a moment to muster up the strength to vocalize the words. He swallowed hard. "Are you saying you lied about the paternity?"

"What?" The expression in her eyes was unreadable. "Is that what you're hoping?"

"No. But if you're refusing the paternity test, there has to be a reason. And the only one that I can think of is you lied to me."

"Or the fact that you totally misunderstood my answer."

He sighed and rubbed the back of his neck. He never knew talking with a woman could be this complicated, but then again, he'd never let his relationships get serious. All his conversations since Abree had been flirting and casual talk about his travels. His whole future had never been on the line.

"Does that mean you agree to the test? It's the only way we can become a family and put the child in line for the throne."

"It means that no matter what is revealed by

the test, we are *not* getting married. And I'm not becoming a princess."

He processed what she told him, but he wanted to make sure they were on the same page. "So you're agreeing to the test?"

She nodded.

"But you don't want to be my wife."

"Exactly."

"And the child? How do you expect that to work out? Because if it is my child, I will not turn my back on it."

"I... I don't know how things will work out. I haven't had much time to consider it."

"But you're sure you don't want to be a part of the royal family?"

She nodded. "I already have a complicated family. I don't need another. If I marry, it will be for love and nothing less. And you do not love me."

He wanted to argue with her. But he couldn't lie to her. Sure they'd spent some wonderful time together, but he wasn't ready to put his heart on the line.

He'd been raised to do what was expected of him—to put the needs of the royal family ahead of his own. And he was told from a young age that marriage was a business contract and it had nothing to do with romantic fantasies.

However, Max learned from his time on his own that many people held tight to their dreams of love and happily-ever-after. He didn't know why when so many people ended up with a broken heart. There really wasn't such a thing as love. There was respect. There was friendship. That had to be enough.

His gaze moved to Noemi. A glint of determination reflected in her eyes. He knew there was no arguing with her. He needed to show her that they could have a good life together—even if they didn't love each other.

"It's okay," she said. "Why don't we give it some more time to think through our situation? And then we can figure out what makes the most sense."

At last, they could agree on something. "I think that's a good idea. In the meantime, spend the rest of the week with me."

"I… I don't know."

"I don't know how the future will play out, you know, with the baby and all, but I think we should take advantage of our relative privacy here at the resort in order to get to know each other better. Because at the very least, I'm going to be the father of your child."

Noemi silently stared at him as though weighing his words. And then she nodded. "You're right. We should know each other better since we'll be linked for life. But I have one condition."

"And that would be?"

"As long as you don't pressure me about the baby and marriage."

He held up his hand as though he were about to take the oath to the throne. "I swear."

Marry a prince…

Wasn't that every girl's dream?

Noemi longed to talk to her mother. What would her mother tell her? To hold out for love? Or be practical and give the baby a mother and father living under one roof—even if they didn't love each other?

She was torn. Both options had their positives and negatives. But what was best for all of them?

At least Max had heard her and was giving them time to figure this thing out. He had no idea how much it meant to her that he valued her opinion.

Noemi tied her hair back in a short ponytail and pulled a white knit cap down over it. She selected her biggest sunglasses and headed for the door. It'd been a long time since she'd gone tubing and she was looking forward to it.

And it was just as she'd remembered. The sun beaming on her face. The cold air filling her lungs. And her racing to the bottom of the hill. The first trip down, Max had won. The second time down, she'd won.

Noemi walked through the fluffy white snow, feeling like a kid again. No responsibilities. No messy family stuff.

It helped that Max hadn't mentioned the M-word again that day. In fact, he'd kept everything light and casual.

She couldn't remember smiling so much.

But she wasn't a child and neither was Max. He was all man—tall and muscled. His eyes said he'd experienced more in life than most people his age, and yet he was able to have fun with her.

"You have to stop this," Noemi said.

The smile immediately fled his face. "What's wrong? Is it the baby?"

She continued to smile as she shook her head. "The baby is fine. It's my cheeks that are having the problem."

"I don't understand."

"My cheeks are sore from smiling so much."

She glanced at him. "Speaking of cheeks, are you ever going to shave again?"

He ran a hand over his thickening stubble. "You don't like it?"

She pursed her lips and studied him. "I don't know."

"I'm keeping it temporarily. It's part of my disguise."

With things going so well between them, she had an idea. She didn't know what Max would think of it, but it was something she wanted to share with him.

"Hey, I have a doctor's appointment next week and I was wondering if you'd want to go with me?"

His eyes widened. "You mean for the baby?" When she nodded, he asked, "Is anything wrong?"

"No, it's a regular checkup. They're going to do a sonogram and we'll be able to hear the baby's heartbeat."

"Already?" When she smiled and nodded again, he said, "I'd love it. Thank you for asking me."

She never thought she could be this happy. She told herself this feeling wasn't going to last, but a voice in her head said to enjoy this moment as long as it lasted. When it was over, she'd have the memories to cherish.

And then there was Max, Crown Prince Maximilian Steiner-Wolf, who made her stomach dip every time he smiled at her. Not only did they have fun together, but he'd also been there to comfort her through the morning sickness. He was so sweet to insist on making her tea. This prince was something extra special.

"Let's go again." She trudged toward the lift.

"Aren't you hungry?"

She shook her head. Okay. Maybe she was a little hungry, but she wanted to go down the hill one more time. And then she had something special in mind for after lunch.

"Please," she begged. "It'll be a tiebreaker."

He sighed. "How can I say no to that pouty look on your face?"

"Yay!" She grabbed his hand without thinking and pulled him toward the line for the tube lift.

Was it possible she could feel the heat of his body emanating through their gloves? Or was it just a bit of wishful thinking? She should let go of him. But it was so much easier to live in the moment and not think about what the future would bring them.

She tightened her hold on him as they slowly

moved closer to the lift. "Isn't this the most beautiful day?"

Max looked at her and then glanced up at the sky. "Are we looking at the same sky? It's cloudy."

She breathed in deeply. "I can smell snow."

"You can't smell snow."

She nodded. "Can too. It smells fresh and crisp." She inhaled deeply. "It smells like snow."

He smiled and shook his head. "If you say so."

When his gaze connected with hers, her stomach dipped again. "I do."

"Next," the attendant said. He waved her forward.

With great reluctance, she let go of Max's hand. She didn't know why that connection should mean so much to her. It wasn't like they were in love or anything.

They were friends. Nothing more. Well, not quite. They were going to be parents to a little, innocent baby. That was a connection unlike any other. They had to continue to get along for the child. That was the most important part. She didn't want her child growing up in a stressful environment where the parents always argued.

At the top of the small hill, she waited for him to join her. Once they were side by side in their respective tubes, she turned to him. "First one to the bottom gets to pick what we do this afternoon."

"You think you're really going to beat me?"

"I know I am." She took off down the hill.

"Hey…" His voice got lost in the breeze as the first few snowflakes started to fall.

She laughed as the tube glided down over the dips. This was one of the best days of her life. And for the first time since learning she was pregnant, she felt everything was going to work out. She didn't quite know how, but she believed it would work out for the best and her baby would be happy.

She reminded herself not to get too wrapped up in the prince. They were just friends. There were no strings attached. But the harder she tried to resist his charms, the more she fell for the sexy prince.

She tempered her excitement with the knowledge that the people she loved eventually let her down. Max would eventually let her down, too—whether he meant to or not.

CHAPTER SEVEN

"YOU CHEAT."

Max didn't mind losing the race to Noemi—not at all. But he liked teasing her and keeping the smile on her face. She had the most beautiful smile with her rosy lips and it lit up her brown eyes.

"I do not," she said emphatically. "I can't help that you're slow."

"I am not."

There had been nothing slow about his attraction to her at the party that now seemed a lifetime ago. There was nothing slow about the rush of desire that came over him every time she was close by. And there was nothing slow about his yearning to care for her and their unborn child.

They'd just finished lunch in the ski lodge in a private room away from any curious eyes. He worried his beard wouldn't be enough to keep him from being recognized. And he knew he'd stand out if he wore a hat and sunglasses throughout their meal.

And now it was time for him to ante up for losing the tubing race. "So what do you have in mind for the afternoon? Please tell me it isn't skiing."

Her eyes twinkled with mischief. "Well, now that you mention it, skiing doesn't sound so bad—"

"Noemi, you really should be careful—"

"I never would have guessed you'd be a worrier."

"I don't worry. I'm just being cautious. There's a difference."

She shook her head. "Anyway, I've decided to give it up until the baby is born. Better safe than sorry."

"Thank you. So, what did you have in mind for this afternoon?"

She wiped the corners of her mouth with the white linen napkin and pushed aside her empty plate. "I was wondering if you would want to do some shopping with me."

"Shopping?" It was definitely not something he would have suggested. And it was not something he would enjoy. In fact, it was one of the last things he wanted to do. A dentist appointment sounded more appealing.

Noemi frowned. "I can see you don't like the idea."

He'd have to work harder in the future to keep his thoughts from reflecting on his face. "Not at all." He forced a smile. He knew how to be a good loser. "What are we shopping for?"

"I thought we could look at some baby stuff."

Baby stuff? He had absolutely no idea what that would entail. "Where do we have to go?"

"It's right up the road from here. What do you think?" The hopeful look on her face was too much for him to turn down.

"I think we should go. I'll call my driver."

Once the bill was paid, they were out the door. Max's car and two bodyguards were waiting for them. They were quickly ushered into the village, where upscale shops carried most anything you could think of to buy. And there in the heart of the village was a baby boutique.

The boutique was small but that didn't detract from its appeal. Pink, blue and white checked nursery bunting adorned the window, while in the center sat a bassinet, some stuffed animals and itty-bitty clothes. Noemi grinned with excitement. Maybe this surprise baby thing wasn't all so bad. And then her gaze slipped to Max, who opened the shop door for her. No, definitely not so bad at all.

Inside, the shop was brightly lit and filled with pastel colors of every shade. In the background, children's music played. A saleswoman approached them with a smile and offered to assist them, but they waved her off, saying they were just there to look around.

After the woman returned to the checkout, Max turned to Noemi. "We are just looking around, aren't we?"

Noemi shrugged. "It would be so hard not to buy something. It's all so cute. Don't you think?"

It was Max's turn to shrug. She could tell he was trying hard not to be moved by what this shopping trip meant to their future. In less than six months, they were going to have this tiny baby in their arms. He or she would be relying on them for everything. The enormity of the responsibility didn't escape her—in fact, it downright scared her. She'd never been responsible for another human. What if she messed up?

When she'd first learned she was pregnant, she'd considered adoption. She'd quickly dismissed the idea. That's what her parents had been forced to do with Leo and they'd regretted it ever since. She didn't want to be separated from her child. Her hand instinctively moved to the ever-so-slight bump in her midsection. She was already in love.

As she perused a pink, yellow and white dress that looked like it was made for a fine china doll, she couldn't help but feel people staring at them. When she lifted her head, she noticed a young woman had joined the older saleslady at the checkout. She was staring at them. Noemi slipped her sunglasses on and pulled her cap down so it covered all her hair.

"Maybe coming here wasn't such a good idea," Noemi whispered.

"It's fine. My security is by the door. Nothing will happen."

"I think we should go." She worried her bottom lip, but as she looked around this time, she didn't notice anyone staring at them.

"Just keep shopping. Everything is fine."

Perhaps he was right. After all, he was far more familiar with fame than she was. Once off the runway and with her heavy makeup removed, she wasn't easily recognized as the face of Cattaneo Jewels. That used to bother her. Once upon a time, she'd longed for fame.

She used to wear her runway makeup and finest fashions every time she went out. She'd wanted the attention that she failed to get at home. Where her family was concerned, everything had been about Cattaneo Jewels while her opinions were disregarded—while she, as a person, was disregarded.

But ever since she'd learned she was pregnant, her parents had died and Leo had entered her life, being recognized and asked for her autograph had lost its appeal to her. She was learning that there were far more important things in life.

Noemi fingered through the selection of baby clothes. The outfits were all so tiny and adorable. But at this point, she didn't know if she was having a boy or a girl. That would make buying things difficult. But that didn't stop Noemi from leisurely strolling up and down the aisles, feeling the ruffles and placing a pair of booties on her fingertips.

She glanced at Max. "Do you want to know if it's a boy or girl? You know, at the sonogram?"

"Can they tell this soon?"

"I don't know but we can ask." She had a baby book back at the chalet. Maybe it would tell her.

He glanced at the booties dangling from her fingertips. "Can you believe they'll be small enough to wear those?"

"I hope so. Or else I'm in really big trouble." She smiled back at him before turning back to the itty-bitty clothes.

"You're going to be a fantastic mother."

She turned to him and lifted her chin in order to look him in the eyes. "Do you really think so?"

"I do." There was no hesitation in his voice and his gaze did not waver.

"At least one of us thinks so."

His voice lowered. "Trust me."

His gaze lowered to her lips and lingered there. The heat of excitement swirled in her chest before rushing up her neck and warming her cheeks. He was considering kissing her. And even though they'd already spent the night together, everything had changed since then.

His desire for her, was it real? Or was it fleeting? She didn't know. And to be honest, she didn't know what she wanted it to be. She stepped back.

"Oh, look." She rushed over to an entire display of stuffed animals. There were yellow ducks, green frogs, purple hippos, brown monkeys, polka-dotted inchworms and a whole assortment of other creatures. "Aren't they adorable?"

"Why don't you pick one out?"

She shook her head. "I don't think so."

"Why not?"

"Because I couldn't pick just one. They are all so cute."

"Then I will buy them all for you."

She turned to him, hoping he was joking. He wasn't. "Max, you can't."

"Sure, I can. Watch me."

As he went to make his way to the checkout, Noemi reached out and grabbed his arm. "Wait. You're not being reasonable."

"Of course I am. You like them all. Your smile lit up the whole room. I like when you smile like that. I'll buy the stuffed animals so you'll keep smiling."

When he went to pull away from her hold, her fingers tightened on his black wool coat. "Seriously, you can't. What would I do with all of them?"

He paused as though giving her question some serious thought. "Decorate the nursery?"

"There wouldn't be any room left for the crib or changing table."

"I hadn't thought of that. Maybe the baby will have two rooms. One for the practical stuff and one for the fun stuff."

Noemi's smile broadened. "Something tells me you'd actually do that."

"Sure, I would."

"How about, for now at least, we pick out just one stuffed animal for the baby?"

"One?"

She nodded and then turned back to the display that spanned the whole length of the back wall. "What do you think? A puppy? A kitty? A turtle?"

He shook his head. "I shouldn't pick it out. You're the one who fell in love with them."

"So you're making me do the hard job?"

"Just this once."

She didn't argue. It was a tough job, but she was up to the challenge. Then her eyes scanned the top shelf. Each plush creation called out to her. This definitely wasn't going to be easy.

But she was thoroughly excited to pick out their baby's first stuffed animal. It would be a keepsake. A stuffed animal that hopefully her child would still have when they were all grown up. Something to measure the time of her child's life—when they looked at it, they would remember their earliest childhood memories. Her eyes grew misty. She blinked repeatedly.

Oh, boy, were the mommy hormones kicking in full gear. She'd never been this sentimental in her life. But everything was different now.

She was different, but she didn't feel as though she was done changing yet.

The purple snake she skipped over. That was an easy decision. She also crossed off anything pink or blue. Knowing her luck, she'd pick the wrong color.

She didn't know how much time had passed when she heard Max ask, "Do you need some help?"

She shook her head. "I've got this."

She had it narrowed down to a teddy bear, a lion or an elephant. She was tempted to take all three. But then how would she decide which was her child's first stuffed animal? She had to wonder that if something this simple was giving her such great pains to decide, how would she ever make the bigger decisions concerning her child?

Her stomach tightened as she realized the lifetime of responsibilities facing her. And with her parents gone, she wouldn't have anyone to turn to with her questions and doubts. But then she looked over at Max, who was trying so hard not to look bored. At least she wouldn't be all alone with this parenthood thing. Something told her Max would always be available for his child.

She glanced back at the three stuffed animals

in her arms. And she knew right away which one to pick.

"Close your eyes," she said.

"But why?"

"Just do it. Please."

Max sighed. "Okay."

She waited until he'd done it and then she stuffed the other animals back on the shelf. She turned back to Max and said, "Okay. Hold out your hands."

A little smile pulled at his lips as he did what she asked.

She placed the animal in his hands. "Okay. You can open them now."

He opened his eyes and lifted his hands closer to his face. "You picked out a purple lion."

She nodded and smiled.

"And how did you decide on him?"

"I wanted our child's first animal to be something special. The lion will remind them of their father. A lion is king of the jungle, just as you are king of a great nation. The lion is also strong and protective of those he cares about."

"And that's how you see me?" His gaze studied her.

"That's how I see you as a father. Or rather a father-to-be."

She'd dodged that question. Her heart sped

up when she thought of herself belonging to him—of him belonging to her. Realizing her thoughts were gravitating toward dangerous territory, she shoved them to the back of her mind.

Max studied the lion as though pondering her words.

"Shall we go?" she asked.

He glanced up at her with a puzzled look. Had he been so deep in thought that he hadn't heard her? Could her words really have affected him so deeply? Not wanting to make a big deal of it. She repeated her question.

"Sure," he said.

When she reached out for the lion, she noticed the booties in her hand. She wasn't sure what to do with them. She should probably put them back. After all, she could pick out all that stuff once the sex of the baby was determined—

"Get them." Max's voice cut through her mental debate.

She glanced down at them. They were so cute. "Okay."

Noemi followed Max through the narrow aisles to the checkout. All the while, Noemi was admiring her finds. It wasn't until they were at the register and the items were on the counter that flashes lit up the room.

Max turned his back to the store window and pulled her to his chest, shielding her from the probing cameras. What were they going to do if they came inside?

"Oh, my," the older saleslady said.

"Isn't this great?" the younger woman said, all the while her fingers moved rapidly over her phone.

If Noemi was a betting person, she'd hazard a guess that the young woman had alerted the paparazzi to the prince's presence in the shop. And then reality started to settle in—they were in a baby boutique. The whole world was about to know that she was baby shopping with the Prince of Ostania. She inwardly groaned.

"I'm sorry about this," the prince said softly. Over his shoulder, he said to the salesclerk, "Is there a back way out of here?"

The older woman gestured to the back of the shop.

"Come on." With the stuffed animal and booties left behind, Max took Noemi's hand and rushed her out the back while his bodyguard led the way.

But where was the other security guy? There

had been two of them. She glanced around but didn't see him anywhere. How strange.

As they ducked out the back door into a single-lane alley, she realized the other man had gone off to get their vehicle.

They scrambled into the black SUV with tinted windows and set off down the alley just as the photographers rounded the corner. More flashes went off, but it was all right. The back windows were so heavily tinted that it was doubtful they would get a usable photo.

It wasn't until they were away from the press that her muscles began to relax. She leaned her head back against the leather seat. What had just happened?

CHAPTER EIGHT

"I'M SORRY."

Max kept repeating those words the next morning at Noemi's chalet. It was earlier than they'd intended to meet up, but he knew she was already up because she'd texted him, canceling today's plans to go snowmobiling.

He didn't need anyone to tell him the reason for the cancellation. The paparazzi had once again messed with his life. Before it hadn't mattered so much, but now it was jeopardizing his future.

His phone had been ringing since last night, but he had yet to speak with his mother or Enzo. Apparently they'd been apprised of the headlines. He needed time to make a plan before he spoke with either of them.

Noemi turned away from him, hugging her arms across her chest as she sat on the couch in her gray pajama pants and a silky pink robe. Her hair was yanked back in a ponytail holder and her face was pale. "You really shouldn't have come over. I know you have plans."

"Those plans included you. And I needed to check on you." He also had some more bad news to share with her, but he wasn't quite ready to spring it on her just yet.

"I'm fine." Her complexion said otherwise.

"I should have thought more about going into the village." The truth was that he hadn't been thinking about much of anything yesterday except for making Noemi happy. "With our ability to avoid the paparazzi on the ski slopes, I'd hoped they'd grown bored and moved on to another story—another town."

Noemi lifted her gaze to meet his. "Did you really think that would happen?"

"I guess I've grown accustomed to them being on the fringes of my life. Perhaps I got too careless. And I'm sorry you got caught up in the middle of all of it."

There was a definite pause. "It's not your fault."

"You might not feel that way when I show you this." He pulled his phone from his pocket.

"What is it?" Worry lines marred her beautiful face.

It killed him to be the one to cause her such distress. "I'll let you see for yourself."

He pulled up the headline and photo before handing it over to Noemi.

"Crown Prince to Daddy!"

Beneath the headline was a photo of him in the baby boutique. And standing just behind him was Noemi. But her head was turned and the view of her face was partially obstructed by his shoulder. Her ski cap and sunglasses also added to her anonymity.

Below the picture, the caption read, *But who's the baby's mama?*

Max hadn't been surprised to find it in the headlines today. The only thing to surprise him was the fact that Noemi's identity was still a mystery. And that's the way he wanted it to remain.

With great reluctance, he handed over his phone. Immediately Noemi gasped. Her face grew pale. An awkward silence ensued as she read the article summarizing his life and his eventual ascension to the throne.

Over the years, the paparazzi had written many false stories about him, from him eloping to him abdicating his crown to him joining a professional rock band. None of them had even been close to true. But this story, it hit too close to home for his family to ignore.

It would change so much for everyone. And so he needed to return to Ostania immediately.

He didn't want to do that without Noemi. But would she go with him?

She handed his phone back to him. If her face was pale before, now it was a pasty gray. And then without a word, she darted out of the room. He didn't have to ask; he knew the morning sickness had returned.

His body tensed as frustration swept through him. He had to do better in the future. It was his job to protect his family and see to their well-being. If he couldn't care for the mother of his child, how was he ever to look after an entire nation?

It was then that he decided no matter what it took, Noemi would go back to Ostania with him. In that way he could see to her well-being. And while they were there, they could make plans for the future—their future. Because somehow—someway—he intended to marry Noemi.

This couldn't be happening.

Noemi's heart pounded. Ever since the run-in at the boutique, she'd realized the fantasy of her and Max living an ordinary life had been nothing but a dream. They weren't ordinary.

She was an heiress and he was a crown prince. It meant that neither of them would have any privacy—now or ever.

Right now, she needed her stomach to settle. She sat on the cold tile floor of the bathroom and leaned her pounding head against the wall. She thought the morning sickness was behind her, but the stress gave her a headache that started her stomach churning.

There was a tap on the door. "Noemi, are you all right?"

She supposed she had been gone for a while. Usually her morning sickness wasn't this bad. She must look quite a sight, but she knew Max wouldn't leave until he was certain she was all right.

"You can come in."

The door slowly opened. Max stood there with a worried frown. "You don't look so good."

"Thank you. That's what all women want to hear."

"I'm sorry. I just meant—"

"I know what you meant. I was just giving you a hard time."

He moved to the sink, where some fresh towels were laid out. The next thing she knew, he sat down next to her and gently pressed a cold washcloth to her forehead.

"Maybe that will help."

The coldness was comforting—so was having Max by her side. She didn't say it, though. It wasn't good to encourage this relationship unless she was ready to share her life with the world. Yesterday proved that. She didn't want her baby to be fodder for headlines.

And then a worrisome thought came to her. "Did the press follow you here?"

He shook his head. "Do you think I would intentionally do that to you?"

"No. But that doesn't mean it couldn't happen accidentally."

"They've been camping outside the gates of the community where I am staying. Thankfully it has guards. One paparazzo did sneak onto the grounds, but he was quickly dealt with. I was able to sneak out in the back of a neighbor's car covered with a blanket. They didn't even notice me. They were intent on watching my SUV."

She breathed a little easier. "Thank you." Feeling a bit better, she removed the cloth from her forehead. She got to her feet. "Sorry about that."

"You don't have to apologize. I can't even

imagine all the changes your body is going through right now. And then this thing with the paparazzi doesn't help matters."

"At least they don't know who I am."

"Yet."

"You mean they aren't going to give up until they find out what you were doing in the boutique?"

He nodded. "They can be like a dog with a bone. Relentless."

"How do you live like that?" She thought she'd had it bad, but her notoriety was miniscule compared to his. For the most part, she could pick and choose when to engage with the press, but Max didn't have that choice.

He cleared his throat. "Some would say it is something you are born into—something that comes along with the job of being royal. Others would say it's a privilege to have access to the world. I don't know what I'd say. Right now, it is a curse. But I also know from watching my father over the years that the press can be used for good things. I'm just sorry that you're caught up in the middle of all this."

"And that's why I want out." She'd wrestled with this decision a large part of the night. She hadn't realized that she'd made the decision until the words popped out of her mouth.

Max didn't say anything at first. It was as though he wasn't sure he'd heard her correctly. But then his eyes grew darker, like that of a stormy sky.

"You want out of what? Having our baby?"

"No." She crossed her arms. "How could you think that?"

He rubbed the back of his neck. "What am I supposed to think?"

"I want out of this." She waved her hand between the two of them. "I want you to walk away. There's nothing tying you to this baby. No paper trail. I haven't told anyone."

"But you forget the one very important tie—I am the baby's father." His mouth pressed closed in a firm line as the muscle in his jaw twitched.

She turned away from him and pressed her hands against the cool granite of the sink counter. "But if you don't tell anyone, no one will know. We can each go our separate way."

Even though she had turned her back on him, his image was there in the mirror. She couldn't tell what he was thinking, only that he wasn't happy. Well, neither was she. This was not the way she wanted things to work out for herself or her child. But they had to be realistic.

Creating a scandal wouldn't be good for their baby either. She didn't want people pointing their fingers at their child and whispering. She didn't want paparazzi hiding behind bushes and springing out, scaring their son or daughter. She didn't want her life to be any more of a three-ring circus than it already was—even if it meant sacrifices had to be made.

"I'll let you finish up in here." His tone was even with no hint of emotion.

She knew he wasn't that calm—that detached. But he strove to hide it well. It must be something about being born a royal. Her family was not that restrained—that in control.

When the bathroom door shut, Noemi pressed a hand to her stomach. "Well, little one, it looks like I've really made a mess of things now."

CHAPTER NINE

SHE WANTS OUT.

Max knew what she was really saying was that she wanted away from him—away from all the baggage that came with being the crown prince. But what she seemed to fail to realize was that was impossible. That little baby within her was the heir to Ostania. But more than that, Max couldn't walk away from his responsibility to the baby—to Noemi.

They were in this together whether they liked it or not.

He moved to the kitchen, where he grabbed some crackers and brewed some tea. He took the food back to the living room to wait for Noemi. He had to return to Ostania right away and he was still determined to take Noemi with him. He wasn't going to leave her alone to deal with the press by herself. But how was he going to convince her that going with him was for the best?

A few minutes later, Noemi returned to the

living room. Her eyes widened when they met his. It appeared she hadn't expected him to hang around. The other men in her life must not have been as determined to keep Noemi in their lives. It was their loss and his gain.

"I got you some crackers. Maybe they will help." He gestured to the plate and cup on the large coffee table.

"You really didn't have to—"

"I wanted to."

She sat down and sipped the tea. "I'm surprised you're still here."

"Did you really think I would leave without straightening things out between us?"

"I thought that's what we'd done." Her gaze met his. "It's best for everyone if we just part ways now."

He didn't believe her. "Is that what you really think?"

Her gaze lowered. "It is."

Why was she being so stubborn? Surely she didn't believe what she was saying. She was scared. The paparazzi could be intimidating. And he supposed she might be intimidated by his position—though most women had the opposite reaction.

Still, he had to get through to her. He had to jar her out of this fantasy that she could just

JENNIFER FAYE 129

erase him from her life. It wasn't going to happen. He wouldn't let it.

"Noemi, I'm not going anywhere. We're in this together."

She shook her head. "I'll be fine on my own."

"But will our baby be fine without a father?"

Her gaze was still lowered. "Lots of children are raised by a single parent."

"And most don't have a choice. But you do. Our child can have two invested parents."

"But at what cost?" Her gaze at last met his. "My pregnancy will become a front-page scandal. It'll be all over the television and internet. And they'll call it our love child. Your illegitimate heir. Or worse."

"Do people still say illegitimate?" he asked in all honesty. "I don't think it will be the scandal that you imagine."

She shook her head. "You aren't going to change my mind."

Oh, yes, he was. Somehow. Some way.

He had one last plan to bring her to her senses. It was with tremendous trepidation that he said, "Are you better off having lost your parents?"

Immediately the pain reflected in her eyes. "That's not the same thing."

"How so? Don't you think our son or daughter will wonder why their friends have both a mother and a father, but they don't? You don't think it will hurt them? You don't think they will grow up with questions?"

For an extended moment, silence filled the room.

Perhaps he'd been too tough on her. But he just couldn't let Noemi delude herself into thinking that exiling him from her life was for the best. It wouldn't be good for any of them. Least of all their child.

"All right," she said, "you've made your point. But I don't see how this is going to work out."

It was time to get to the reason for his visit. "I have to leave today for Ostania."

"Because of the article about us at the baby boutique?"

"Partly." He had a lot of explaining to do with his family—especially his brother.

"Then there's no rush to figure this out." The worry lines on her face eased a bit.

"I want you to come with me."

"To Ostania?"

He nodded. "Have you ever been there?"

She shook her head as she reached for the crackers. "I've always wanted to visit. It looks like such a beautiful country, but I've just never had the opportunity."

"So this is your chance. Let me show you my world. It will be better than sitting here while the paparazzi scour the area for the mysterious woman in the photograph."

She didn't say anything at first. He took that as a positive sign. The longer she was quiet, the more confident he became that she would accompany him to Ostania.

Just then, her phone chimed. She frowned as she read the text message. She responded. Once she set her phone aside, she glanced at Max. There was still a hint of worry written on her face.

"Is everything all right?"

She sighed. "It was my brother Leo. He was letting me know that he has flown back to New York."

"So it's just you in Mont Coeur?"

She nodded. "Until Christmas."

"Then there's no reason for you to stay here alone." Feeling that she might need a little more encouragement, he said, "You can do as much sightseeing or as little as you like. You can consider it a vacation. And we'll be able to get to know each other better."

"But won't you be busy with your duties?"

He would be. He wouldn't lie to her about it. This baby would mean so many things would change. He would be taking on a lot of responsibility that previously had been given to his brother. He had many things to learn about governing a nation.

"I will be busy. It's unavoidable. But I promise you'll have plenty to do. Every amenity is at the palace. And there will be a car at your disposal should you want to go anywhere."

She finished the last cracker. "You make it sound like a relaxing trip to a five-star spa."

"It can be if that's what you'd like."

A look came over her face as though she'd just recalled something. "I can't go. I have a doctor's appointment."

The one where he was supposed to hear his son or daughter's heartbeat and see their image. A pang of regret hit him with the force of a sledgehammer.

"You can't miss that."

A look of relief came over her. "I agree."

"But you could see the doctor in Ostania." When she started to shake her head, he said, "Sure you can."

"It's not that easy. I can't just go strolling into a new doctor's office."

"I can put the doctors in touch with each other. Or I can fly in your doctor."

"You know how to exaggerate a house call."

"I'm a prince. There's a lot I can do. Trust me."

She fidgeted with the hem of her shirt. "You aren't going to let this go, are you?"

He shook his head. "If you stay here, so do I."

"But your family—"

"Will have to wait. This is more important."

"I'm not ready to face your family and discuss the baby. We…" she waved her hand between them "…need to figure things out before we tell people."

"I agree." By the widening of her eyes, he could see that his response surprised her. "For the moment, we'll keep the fact that the baby is mine between us."

They sat there quietly staring at each other. If she was trying to find another reason not to go on this trip, he would continue to find ways to allay her worries. He would do whatever it took to ensure the safety of the mother of his baby.

Noemi expelled a sigh and pressed her hands to her hips. "If I do this—if I go with you—I have to return to Mont Coeur for Christmas as my family has some matters to sort out."

"Understood." It sounded like she'd just agreed to travel to Ostania with him, but he wanted to be absolutely certain. "So you'll accompany me?"

She nodded. "I just need to get packed."

"Do you need help?"

She shook her head.

"I'll wait here." He sat down and pulled out his phone. "Just let me know if you need anything. And don't lift the suitcase. I'll get it."

She didn't say anything else as she turned for her room. He couldn't tell if she was angry or just resigned. He hoped with a little time and some rest that she would see this arrangement was for the best.

Had she made the right decision?

Noemi smothered a yawn. It was too late to change her mind as the private jet soared above the puffy white clouds. Part of her said that she should have stayed back at the chalet and hibernated until the press gave up their search for the mysterious woman in the photo. But another part of her wasn't ready to let go of Max—of the dream that their baby could be part of both of their lives.

There was something special about him. It was there when he smiled at her and made her stomach dip. And there was the way he looked at her that made her feel like she was the only woman in the world. And then there was his gentleness and kindness.

Not that she was falling for him or anything.

She refused to let herself do that. She'd agreed to fly to Ostania because it was best for the baby to have parents who were good friends—who could work together to raise a happy and healthy child. Nothing more.

Noemi continued to stare out the window as the plane descended, preparing to land at the private airstrip somewhere near the Ostania palace—at least that's what Max had said when he'd told her to fasten her seat belt. Even though the sun was sinking low in the sky, she was able to make out the palace. The sight captured her full attention. This was where Max lived? *Wow!*

Even from this height, it looked impressive with its blue turrets and white walls. She couldn't even imagine calling this place home. It looked like an entire village could fit within its walls and still have some extra room for visitors.

With so much space, it made her wonder why Max had felt the need to leave here for so long. What had he been running from? Was it his parents? Were they overbearing? She hoped not. Second thoughts about this trip started to niggle at her.

Nestled in the jagged snow-covered mountains, she had no idea where they were going to land. But the plane kept descending and soon a small clearing came into view with a runway. All around the cleared airstrip was snow. It certainly wasn't large enough for a commercial jet. In fact, it seemed rather short—

The wheels touched down with a jolt. Her fingers tightened on the armrests. She closed her eyes and waited. They would stop in time. Wouldn't they?

"Are you okay?" Max asked, drawing her from her thoughts.

As the plane rolled to a stop, she expelled a pent-up breath. "Yes. Um…why?"

"It's just that you've been quiet the entire flight."

She shrugged. "I just have a lot on my mind."

"I understand."

Did he? Did he know how hard this was going to be for all of them? And what was his family going to say when they heard about the baby? But then again, they probably already heard the rumors that had been in the newspaper.

"What about your family?" she asked.

"What about them?"

"They must have heard the gossip. Are you going to confirm their suspicions that the baby is yours?"

He shook his head. "Not until you're ready.

They know after my cancer treatments that children are unlikely. They'll easily dismiss the story as nothing but fiction."

She hoped he was right because this pregnancy was becoming more complicated with each passing day.

They were ushered into a waiting black sedan with the flags of Ostania waving on each front fender. She received surprised looks from everyone she met, but none of them vocalized their thoughts. It would appear Prince Max didn't make it a practice of bringing women home with him. She took comfort in the knowledge.

The car moved slowly over the snow-covered road. Noemi told herself the poor road conditions were the reason her stomach was tied up in knots. It had nothing to do with wondering if Max's family would like her or not.

Max reached out, placing his hand over hers. "Relax. My family is going to love you."

She turned a surprised look at him. How had he known what she was thinking?

"I don't know. I'm not royal. In fact, I don't have a clue how to address your mother and father."

"Don't make a big deal of it."

She sat up a bit straighter. As the car drew

closer to civilization, she grew more nervous. "I'm serious. What do I do? Curtsy?"

Max laughed. It was a deep warm sound and it helped calm her rising nerves. "I don't think that will be necessary."

"But I need to do something."

"How about a slight bow and a nod of your head?"

"Really? Because I don't want to do anything to offend them."

Surprised reflected in Max's eyes. "You really care that much?"

"Shouldn't I?" Even if they weren't Max's parents and the grandparents of her baby, she'd want to make a good impression. After all, they were king and queen. Wait until she told Stephania and Maria about all this.

Their car approached a small village that was nestled in a valley while the palace sat partway up the mountain in the background. The palace glowed like a jewel as floodlights illuminated it in the darkening evening.

But down here in the village, rooftops were covered with snow. And in the center of the village was an enormous Christmas tree. It soared up at least two stories. And it was lit with white twinkle lights. The branches were dusted with snow. It was simple and yet at the same time, it was stunning.

Noemi longed to stay here in the village. There was nothing intimidating about it, unlike the palce. As the car slowly passed through the center of the village, all the pedestrians turned. Men removed their hats and covered their hearts while the women waved. With the tinted windows, they couldn't make out who was in the back seat but they waved nonetheless. Noemi resisted the urge to wave back.

"Do they always do that?" she asked, curious about Ostania and its people.

"Yes. And under different circumstances, I'd stop and greet them."

And then Noemi felt bad. "You won't stop because of me."

"Correct." He didn't elaborate.

He didn't have to. She already knew her condition was changing their lives. What would his family do when he told them about the baby? Would they demand they marry?

Her body stiffened at the idea of a marriage of convenience. If she ever married, it would be for love and nothing less.

But she was pregnant with the prince's child. A royal baby could change things. Would they try to force her?

No. Of course not. It wasn't like she was a citizen of Ostania. They had no power over her. She glanced over at Max as he stared out the window. He wouldn't let his parents force them into anything that they didn't want. She trusted him.

That acknowledgment startled her. She'd never really thought about it before, but she did trust him. That was the first step in a strong friendship, right?

Max turned to her. "Did you say something?"

"Um, no."

"If you have any questions, feel free to ask. I'll try to answer them or I'll find the answers."

She had a feeling he wasn't talking about their unique relationship but rather her magnificent surroundings and the history of the palace. "Thanks. I'll keep that in mind."

As the palace drew closer, she practically pressed her face to the window as she tried to take in the enormity of the structure. She gazed up at one of the towers and couldn't help but think of Rapunzel. Her hair would have been so long to reach the ground.

She smiled at the memory of the fairy tale. But she couldn't help it. She felt as though a book had been opened and she was about to step into the pages of a real-life fairy tale. And she had absolutely no idea how it was going to end. Her stomach shivered with nerves again.

"Relax. My parents aren't that bad."

"That bad?" Her voice rose a little. "You really know how to put a person at ease."

Max sent her a guilty smile as he took her hand in his. "You know what I mean."

"Uh-huh. Sure. They are going to hate me."

Max squeezed her hand. "It will be fine. I'll be right next to you the whole time."

Her stomach grew uneasy. *Oh, no. Not now.* She reached for her purse and pulled out a packet of crackers.

Max frowned. "Maybe this wasn't such a good idea. I thought I'd be rescuing you from the stress of the press, but it appears the thought of my family is just as bad."

She quickly munched on a couple of crackers.

"Is it helping?" Max gave her long hard look. When she nodded, he said, "Maybe I should have some."

"You're nervous?"

"Let's just say my father might be king of the nation but my mother runs the family. She has definite ideas of how things should work and this thing between us won't fit neatly into her expectations."

Noemi reached for another cracker. "I knew it. She's going to hate me."

"Would you quit saying that? It's just going to take a bit of adjusting on everyone's part."

"Especially when you tell her that we're not getting married."

This time Max didn't say a word. Not one syllable. He turned his head away as the car pulled to a stop in front of the palace.

With great reluctance, Noemi stuffed the remaining crackers back in her purse. Then she ran a finger around the outside her lips, checking for crumbs. The last thing she needed was to meet the king and queen looking a mess. But she had a feeling they'd be more interested in her relationship with Max than her appearance. And then a thought came to her.

"You did tell them you were bringing me, didn't you?"

CHAPTER TEN

ONCE AGAIN, MAX didn't say a word. He continued to stare blindly out the window. He hadn't told anyone about Noemi accompanying him home. Not his mother. Not even Enzo.

Telling them about Noemi would involve questions—questions he wasn't ready to answer. So maybe he'd failed to disclose a couple of things to his parents about his return—a couple of big things. But who could blame him under the circumstances?

It was such a tangled mess. And in the end, his family would insist on an immediate paternity test followed by a wedding, and that last part was a sticking point with Noemi. He had to handle this very carefully or she would bolt. And he couldn't let that happen.

"Max, you did tell them, didn't you?"

Before he could answer, both of their car doors swung open. He let go of her hand as he stepped out of the car. When he turned toward the palace, Enzo was standing there, and next to him was the queen. *Oh, boy!* She didn't normally greet him at the door.

Max straightened his shoulders and moved to Noemi's side. He presented his arm to her, in proper royal fashion, and escorted her up the few steps to the sweeping landing.

"Your Highness." He nodded in recognition of his mother's station—etiquette was something his parents had instilled in both him and his brother from a young age.

"Maximilian." The queen continued to frown at him. "It's about time you came home."

She was the only one to call him by his formal name. Not even his father, the king, called him that. But his mother was all about pomp and circumstance. He rarely ever saw his mother with her hair down, literally or figuratively. When he became ruler, things would change—they would be less rigid. But all that hinged on Noemi…

Not only did he have to sire an heir, but that heir must reside within the palace and be groomed from birth to take over the reins of the Ostania. There was no room for a modern arrangement of partial custody or holiday visitation. His child must remain here in Ostania with him. And he already knew Noemi would balk at the idea.

His mother's frown deepened. "What is that mess on your face?"

He smiled, knowing his mother abhorred beards. "I thought I'd try something different."

"Well, you're home now. Please shave." The queen turned to Noemi. "And who is this?"

Oh, yes, where were his manners? It was just that being home again after being gone since last Christmas had him a bit off-kilter. His relationship with his mother had always been a bit strained. He got along with his father so much better.

"Mother, I would like to introduce you to Noemi Cattaneo of Cattaneo Jewels." He turned to Noemi. "And this is my mother, Queen Marguerite."

He noticed the surprise reflected in Noemi's eyes when he mentioned her family's business, but that's how things were done within the palace. People weren't just recognized for who they were but what they represented. And Max knew his mother had commissioned a few special pieces from Cattaneo Jewels.

The frown lines etching his mother's ivory complexion eased a bit. "You are related to the owners?"

Noemi nodded. "My parents...started the

business. And now, erm, my brothers and I run the business."

The queen's eyes widened. "How truly interesting. I'd like to hear more later." Then his mother turned back to him. "You did not mention you'd be bringing a guest."

"I didn't?" He knew how to play his mother's games as well as she. "I thought I had."

"No. You didn't." She turned to Enzo. "Did he?"

"Not that I recall, ma'am. But the phone connection wasn't the best. Perhaps I missed it."

Max couldn't help but smile at Enzo's attempt to play the impartial party. The man practically had it down to a fine science. When Enzo's gaze caught the slight smile on Max's face, the man refused to react. However, Max would be hearing more about this later.

"Mother, it's cold out. Shouldn't we go inside?"

The queen hesitated for a moment. Max knew his mother didn't like to be pushed around or have something pulled over on her. She liked to know things before everyone else.

And when she found out what was afoot, he honestly didn't know if she'd be overjoyed with the prospect of a grandchild that no one ever thought was possible or if she'd be outraged that his wild lifestyle had led to a child out of wedlock, to a commoner no less. With his mother, anything was possible. But when the time was right, the first person he had to tell was his brother—Tobias's life was about to be turned upside down.

At last, his mother nodded and turned for the door. It was then that Max glanced over at Noemi. Her face was pale and drawn as she wore a plastered-on smile. He thought the first meeting with his mother had gone rather well considering. But perhaps he should have taken time to warn Noemi that his mother wasn't the warm and fuzzy type. The queen loved her sons. He never doubted it. But she kept her feelings under wraps.

He clearly recalled awakening after his cancer surgery. The room had been dim and he had been a bit disoriented at first. He hadn't moved while gaining his bearings. And then he'd heard the soft cry of someone.

He recalled how his mother been leaning near him. Her head had been resting on his bed with her face turned away. And then she'd said a prayer for him. He'd never been more touched in his life—well, that was until he heard Noemi tell him that he was going to be a father. Those were the two most stunning moments in his life.

He understood that his mother had been raised to keep an outward cool indifference. But he wanted more for his life—for his child's life. He needed his child to never question his fierce love for them.

This had to be some sort of dream.

This just couldn't be real.

The grandmother of her baby was a queen. Noemi's stomach quivered yet again. And from all Noemi could gather, the woman didn't like her and they didn't even know each other yet. Panic set in. Noemi didn't even want to think about what the woman would say when she learned of the baby. Maybe it was best that she never did.

That was it. Noemi would leave right away. She just had to get Max alone. Surely he had to see that coming here was a mistake. She didn't know one thing about royalty. Sure, she'd done an internet search when she'd been alone at night, but she hadn't found much insight. Certainly nothing to prepare her for this.

Once inside the palace, Noemi stopped in the grand foyer. The breath caught in her throat as she took in the magnificent surroundings.

The tiled floor glimmered as the lights from the enormous crystal chandelier reflected off it. The tiles were laid in a diamond pattern of sky blue and black tile.

To either side of the very spacious room were twin staircases with elaborate wrought-iron bannisters with gold handrails. Her attention was drawn back to the center of the room where the chandelier hung prominently. It must have been at least four meters wide with a thousand individual crystals. And straight ahead were four white columns with gold trim. In the center was a large window and between the side columns were archways leading to other parts of the palace.

Off to the side stood a stately Christmas tree. Noemi craned her neck as she looked up at the star at the tippy top. She'd guess the thing stood at least thirty feet tall. *Wow!* And she'd thought the twelve-foot trees that her father used to get for the chalet were tall. They were nothing compared to this tree.

The royal Christmas tree was adorned with white twinkle lights. And the decorations were of white porcelain. All looked to be painstakingly positioned on the tree. They no doubt had professional decorators take care of all the details.

At the chalet, the decorations on the tree had been collected over the years. Some were handmade by her and Sebastian. Other ornaments were from vacations or represented special moments in their lives. Each of her family's ornaments held a meaning whereas this palace tree, though magnificent, didn't seem to bear the weight of the memories and sentiments of Max's family.

For some reason, that made her sad. Surely there had to be another tree somewhere in the palace where they hung their treasured ornaments. Right?

"Noemi?" Max sent her a strange look, jarring her back to the present.

"Yes. Sorry." Heat rushed to her cheeks as she realized she hadn't been paying attention to what Max was saying.

"This is my father, King Alexandre."

The king? She swallowed hard. What was she supposed to do? Bow? Curtsy? Her stomach took that moment to become queasy once again. She wished she could reach in her purse and pull out the remaining crackers, but that would have to wait.

Not sure what to do, she bowed. "Your Majesty."

She hoped she'd got it right. When she straightened, the king drew closer. He was smiling, unlike his wife, who kept a serious look on her face.

The king held out his hand. He was going to shake her hand? She didn't know that kings did such a thing.

He continued to smile at her. "It's so nice to meet one of my son's friends."

"It...it's nice to meet you, too."

He released her hand. "A friend of Max's is a friend of mine."

"Thank you." Was that the right response? Honestly she'd met a lot of rich and famous people, but none of them had ruled their own country. And none of them had been Max's parents. And like it or not, she wanted to make a good impression. So far she hadn't impressed the queen, but she was doing much better with the king. That was at least a step in the right direction. Maybe she wouldn't rush back to Mont Coeur...just yet.

"Have you known my son long?"

"We met a few months ago," Max said.

His father glanced at him and Max grew silent.

Noemi wasn't sure how his father would take to hearing his son was partying it up so she said, "We met via some mutual friends. And we immediately hit it off."

"Immediately?" Max asked.

She turned to Max, not sure what to say.

"As I recall," Max continued, "you weren't so easily swayed to give me a chance."

"I, uh…" What was he doing? Was he trying to give his father a bad impression of her?

"Relax," Max said, "my parents can respect your selectiveness. And since you didn't recognize me, I was just one of your many admirers."

Heat rushed to her face. She felt as though her face were on fire. If Max was trying to smooth things over with his father, he wasn't doing a good job. She wished he would stop speaking.

"He's not serious," Noemi said, clarifying things. "We started to talk and soon we became friends."

"Friends?" Max wore an amused look. When she turned a pointed look at him, he said, "Yes, friends. We've been enjoying the snow. And I thought Noemi would enjoy seeing where I lived."

His father was still smiling, but she could see the wheels in his mind turning. He was wondering what exactly was going on between them. Were they just a casual thing? Or was it something more serious?

She didn't have any answers for him because she didn't have any answers for herself. Only time would tell how things would play out for them and the baby.

"Well, we are glad you've come for a visit," the king said. "Isn't that right, Josephine?"

There was a pause before the queen spoke. "Yes, it is. And someone will show you to your suite so you can settle in while we speak privately with our son."

"Thank you for having me," Noemi said, realizing that she'd been dismissed.

As she glanced to the left, she noticed a staff member waiting for her at the bottom of the steps. She turned back to find the king and queen walking away.

"Don't worry," Max leaned over and whispered in her ear. "Everything is going to work out. I'll catch up with you in a bit."

Noemi hoped he was right. So far she was pretty certain coming here was a mistake, even if his father had been very nice to her. And what were they doing now? Talking about the scandalous headlines? Discussing her pregnancy?

She wondered if she should insist on being

a part of the conversation if it was going to be about her. When she paused and glanced over her shoulder, they were gone now—down some long hallway or behind some closed door. Maybe it was for the best that she hadn't caught up with them.

She continued up the steps. The thought of lying down for a bit sounded so appealing. She had never been this tired in her life. Usually she was a bundle of energy. But not lately. This pregnancy was taking a lot out of her.

And then there was her uneasy stomach. Her hand reached for her purse, anxious to retrieve the crackers, but then she returned her hand to her side. There was no way she was going to trail cracker crumbs through the palace. She'd waited this long, a little longer wouldn't matter.

All the while, she wondered what Max's parents were saying. She knew she needed to trust Max, but being here in this palace, it changed things. It drove home the power and wealth of Max and his family.

He should tell them.

He wanted to. Max couldn't wait to shout it from the towers that he was going to be a father. But he knew Noemi wasn't ready for the pressure or expectations that would bring to her life. For now, he had to protect her.

His country was steeped in archaic traditions, as were his parents. Max didn't agree with most of those traditions, but he wasn't in a position to change them—not yet. For now, he had to go along with what was expected of him, producing an heir and providing a paternity test. When he became king—when his authority could not be disputed—then he could implement changes.

Max stepped into the library and stopped, finding that it wasn't just his parents that wanted to speak to him. There were the two highest members of the royal cabinet as well as Enzo and their public representative. This felt more like the beginning of an inquisition than a homecoming.

From the doorway, he took a moment to really look at his parents. His mother looked much the same. She still had a trim figure, and she had no gray hairs but he had a feeling she had them discreetly covered up. His father, on the other hand, looked older and frailer. His face looked weathered and his eyes were dull. He was sicker than he was willing to admit.

The king stepped forward. "This is the woman, isn't it?"

Max sent him a confused look. It was like he'd stepped into the middle of a conversation and everyone expected him to know what had been said. He refused to be put on the defensive. He'd been in that awkward position too many times in recent years.

"The woman?" he asked.

"Don't do this." His mother stepped up next to his father. "I know we've given you a lot of freedom after your...your illness. Perhaps in hindsight it was too much freedom. It wasn't like we turned a blind eye to your activities. But honestly, the headlines have been getting worse and worse. And now you bring home this girl—"

"She's not a girl. She's a woman. And her name is Noemi."

The queen crossed her arms over her proper navy-and-white linen dress. "I suppose she's the one who claims to be pregnant?"

"Since when did you start believing the headlines? You know what the doctor said. I can't father any children."

The angry look on his mother's face deflated. "So it's not true? There's no baby?"

"Whatever they printed in the paper is nothing but make-believe. There's nothing serious between Noemi and me. We're...friends.

She's really nice. I wish you would give her a chance."

The queen eyed him carefully. "She's important to you?"

He had to be careful here. "She's a good friend. And she's been through a lot lately. I want this visit to go well for her."

His statement only increased his mother's curiosity. "Been through what?"

"Darling, leave Max alone." The king spoke in a congenial tone. "He is home just like you wanted. Let's not rush him back out the door."

His mother hated it when they ganged up on her. "Am I not allowed to be curious about my son and his friends?"

"Of course," the king said. "But you don't have to make it sound like the inquisition."

His mother's eyes lit up as she glared at his father. "Fine. You deal with this. And when it blows up in our faces, it'll be on you." And then she turned back to Max. "Make sure you shave before dinner."

And with that his mother turned and left the room along with the other dignitaries. The door made a resounding thud.

His father shook his head before turning back to Max. "Your mother, she means well. She missed you. I wish you wouldn't stay away for such extended periods."

"I'm sorry, Father. It's just—"

"Easier. I know."

Max nodded. That's what he loved most about his father—his way of understanding him. Whereas his mother was fierce in her love and need to protect the family, his father was the opposite and let his love flow freely and without restriction. For being two opposite types, Max was impressed by the way his parents were able to make their marriage work and last.

"However, I agree with your mother. This woman, she is more than a friend." When Max went to dispute the claim, his father raised his hand to stop him. "Perhaps you don't even see it yourself. But you will. Trust me. It's in the way you look at her and the way you speak of her. However, I'm not so sure she feels the same way as you. So please be careful."

It was no wonder his father was the king. He could see straight through a situation to the heart of the problem—just as he had done now with Max and Noemi.

When his father was called away on urgent business, Max headed for the steps leading upstairs. He wanted to make sure Noemi was comfortably situated. As he walked, his father's words kept rolling around in his mind. Was it that obvious that Noemi wasn't into him?

And if that was the case, what did he do about it? Separate the mother from the child? The thought turned his stomach. There had to be a better way. Pay her to stay here with him and the child until their son or daughter was grown? Again, he didn't like the idea. What did that leave him? To make her fall in love with him?

Max paused outside her door. He swallowed down his thoughts. He didn't want her to sense his inner turmoil. He had to keep it all inside until he figured the best course of action for all concerned—especially their baby.

Knock. Knock.

"Come in." Noemi's voice was faint.

He opened the door and found Noemi sitting up on the bed. Her face was pale and she didn't meet his gaze. He pushed the door closed and rushed to her side. He knelt down in front of her. "Are you all right?"

She nodded. "I felt a little wiped out and I closed my eyes for a few minutes. I guess I fell asleep."

"I didn't mean to wake you."

"It's okay. I don't want to sleep the evening away or else I won't sleep tonight."

"Dinner will be at seven. Will you be up for it?"

She mustered a smile, but it didn't quite reach her eyes. "I'll be fine. By tomorrow, I'll be good as new."

Somehow he didn't quite believe her. The stress of the press compounded by his mother's cold welcome couldn't have helped Noemi's pregnancy. He was going to have to do better. He wanted Noemi to enjoy this visit. He wanted her to fall in love with his country—their child's birthright.

"What would you like to do this evening?" he asked. If it was within his power, he would give her whatever she wanted.

"Would you mind if we didn't do anything?"

That didn't sound like much fun, but he understood that she was tired after their earlier travels. "Not a problem." And then he had an idea. He checked the time and then turned back to her. "We have a little time before dinner, how about I give you a tour of the palace?"

She perked up a bit. "That would be nice."

"Would you like to change now or after the tour?"

"Change?" She sent him a puzzled look.

"For dinner." His mother insisted on formalities, even when it was just the family...and a very special friend.

Worry reflected in her eyes. "Exactly how dressed up do I need to be?"

"Don't worry. If you didn't bring anything to wear for dinner, it'll be fine."

"Of course I brought dressier clothes." She frowned at him. "I do know my way around society, you know."

That was true. She was a Cattaneo. He had worried for nothing. He nodded in understanding. "The men will be wearing suits. So a dress, if you have one, will work."

"I do. I'll change first. That way if the tour takes longer than imagined, I won't hold dinner up while I'm changing."

"Great idea. I'll go and change, too." He ran a hand over his beard. "I guess I'll shave, too. Kind of a shame. It was starting to get past the itchy phase." And with that he was out the door.

Was his father right? Noemi didn't act like the other women who had passed through his life. They were all too eager to be near him, to kiss him, to touch him.

Noemi wasn't that way. She was reserved.

And though in part that should be a relief to him, there was another part that worried that she truly wasn't into him—that all they'd ever have was that one night. And that just wasn't enough for him.

CHAPTER ELEVEN

ACTING ALOOF WAS hard work.

Noemi assured herself that playing it cool was the best way to go. Being here at the palace and after meeting the queen, Noemi was certain she and Max didn't belong together. They came from totally different worlds.

And then she had the worst thought. The queen already seemed not to care for her. When the queen learned of the baby, what if she decided, with them being unmarried, that it would be best to have the baby sent away—put up for adoption—like her parents had been forced to do with Leo?

Noemi's imagination had a way of getting away from her. It was only when she reined it in that she realized an adoption would never happen. She and Max were in a totally different position from her parents. Noemi and Max weren't kids. They didn't rely on their parents for food and shelter. They could make up their own minds.

It was just her nervousness from being here. She glanced around the room. It was large with high ceilings and gold trim work. The landscape paintings on the walls were stunning. She moved closer to them. Each painting contained bright-colored wildflowers. In one painting, the wildflowers were part of a big field with blue skies and puffy white clouds overhead. In another painting, the flowers were next to a pond with a white swan. And the last painting was of the wildflowers with the palace in the distance.

Her initial thought was to move to the window next to her bed to look out and search for the beautiful wildflowers, but in the next instance, she recalled that it was Christmastime and the ground was covered with snow. It would be many months before the wildflowers were to bloom again. And by the time they did, Noemi would have given birth to her baby and she would not be welcome at the palace.

Still, she couldn't resist glancing out the window. As she peered out the window, her mouth gaped. Max had his very own ice skating rink.

"Wow."

This place was just mind-blowing. It was more a private resort than a home. As she stared down at the ice, it beckoned to her. She'd been skating since she was a kid and she loved it. She wondered if Max knew how to skate.

Realizing that she was losing track of time, Noemi turned from the window. Her gaze scanned the room searching for her luggage. The suitcases weren't sitting on the floor. In fact, they were nowhere to be seen. How could that be?

Perhaps they were in the bathroom. She moved to the adjoining bath. The room was practically the same size as her bedroom. And on one wall was a line of cabinets. Was it possible they were in there?

She opened the first door and found it empty, but the second door she opened revealed her clothes. Someone had taken the time and trouble to hang her things up. That was so nice of them. She would have to remember to thank them.

She examined each of her dresses, trying to decide which one the queen might approve of. By the time she'd gone through them all twice, she was no closer to a decision. In the end, she picked a little black dress. It wasn't too flashy. And it wasn't too casual. And most of all, it wasn't too tight around her rapidly expanding midsection.

Not too bad. She glanced at her image in the mirror. *But not too great either.*

She couldn't help but notice the paleness of her face. And were those dark circles under her eyes? She sighed and turned back to the bed, where she'd scattered her things while searching for some concealer.

She'd learned long ago how to make herself presentable in a rush. When she was rushing from the stage to an after-party, there wasn't much time to waste. And when photos were being taken at the parties to distribute to the press, she had to look her best. After all, she was the face of Cattaneo Jewels. It was important to her to do her duty for the family business. She took her responsibility seriously. But perhaps she'd rushed too much today because she couldn't find her elusive makeup.

She didn't know why she was a ball of nerves. It wasn't like her. She was normally confident about her appearance. But that extra two or three inches on her waistline was knocking her confidence. At least that's what she kept telling herself. It had nothing to do with the fact that Max had been keeping a respectable distance from her.

His only interest appeared to be in the baby she was carrying. She tried telling herself that was a good thing. A baby was enough of a complication in her life. She didn't need a prince to mix up her world further. But it didn't keep her from wanting more.

By the time Max rapped his knuckles on her door, Noemi was dressed, her hair was straightened into a smooth bob and she'd at last located her makeup. It wasn't until she looked in the mirror that she realized she'd forgotten her jewelry, which she found ironic as she was now an owner of an international jewel company.

She yanked open the door. "Did you know there's a great big ice skating rink out there?"

Max laughed. "Yeah, I knew. If I'd have known you would get so excited about it, I would have brought you here much sooner."

"It's just that we never got to ice skate back at Mont Coeur." And then realizing that if they didn't hurry they'd be late for dinner, Noemi added, "I hope this dress is all right."

"All right?" His gaze skimmed down over her, warming her skin. "You look amazing."

The heat moved to her face. "Thank you."

She couldn't help but notice his clean-shaven face. Was it possible he looked more princely now? The black suit that spanned over his broad shoulders and cloaked his sculpted biceps looked quite dashing on him. A black tie and white shirt obscured her view of his chest with the smattering of curls that she so fondly remembered.

Realizing that she was letting her thoughts get away from her, she jerked her gaze back up to meet his. "And you're looking rather amazing, too." And then another thought came to her. "Does your family dress formally for every meal or is it just dinner?"

"For breakfast and lunch, it's casual. But my mother insists people dress for dinner. I take it your family isn't so formal?"

She shook her head. "My parents were casual at home. They…" Her voice caught in the back of her throat. She missed them so much. "They were more concerned about getting the family together than anything else."

"It sounds like your family is very close."

Her thoughts turned to her brothers. One was growing more distant by the day and the other one she was hoping to get to know. Not quite the definition of closeness.

She noticed Max watching her as though waiting for an answer. She swallowed down the lump of emotion. "We used to be—at least I thought we were."

But was that truly the case? Had she only seen what she wanted to? After all, her parents had lied to her all her life. The acknowledgment stabbed at her heart. That was not the definition of a close family.

Her thoughts turned to her baby. She would do better by it. She wouldn't lie to it. Never about the big stuff. And she'd listen to him or her—really listen.

"Noemi?"

She blinked. And then she glanced up at Max. Deciding to turn their conversation back to a safer subject, she said, "Perhaps after this evening, I could eat in my room."

Max's brows drew together. "Why would you do that? Is it my mother? If so, I'll have a word with her. She can come on a bit strong."

Noemi shook her head. "It isn't her." Although his mother's disapproving stare did make her uncomfortable, Noemi wasn't one to back down. "If you must know, I don't fit in most of my dresses any longer. They don't hide my expanding baby bump."

A slow smile pulled at Max's tempting lips. "Is that all?" When she nodded, he said, "Then tomorrow we shall take you dress shopping and you can pick up anything else that you need... or want."

"But do you think that's wise?" When he sent her a puzzled look, she added, "You know, after the paparazzi spotted us at the baby boutique in Mont Coeur."

"Let me worry about the paparazzi."

Who was she to argue? She already had her share of worries. "I just don't want to be a bother."

"That's an impossibility." He smiled at her—a genuine smile, the kind that lit up his whole face including his eyes.

Oh, boy, is he handsome.

Her stomach dipped. No man had ever made her feel that way with just a smile. She'd have to be careful around him or she'd end up leaving her heart in Ostania and that wouldn't be good for either her or the baby.

Max checked the time. "Shall we go? We have just enough time to visit a couple of rooms before we are expected in the great dining hall."

"So this isn't going to be a small intimate dinner in the kitchen?" Somehow facing the queen in a more relaxed setting seemed so much more appealing.

Max shook his head. "I'm not even sure my mother has ever been in the kitchen. I know my father has as I would run into him when I was a kid in the middle of the night searching for a snack."

Noemi smiled. She liked the fact that the

king was so much more approachable. Now if only she could find a way to win over the queen. She wondered if that was even possible.

Max once again presented his arm to her. She really liked his old-world charm. Whoever said that manners were outdated hadn't met Max. He made everything relevant.

Her gaze moved from his clean-shaven face to his extended arm and then back again. Without a word, she slipped her hand in the crook of his arm.

She couldn't deny the thrill she got from being so close to him—from feeling the heat of his body emanating through the dark material. Her heart picked up its pace. It'd be so easy to get caught up in this fairy tale… A snowy palace and she the damsel on the crown prince's arm as they set off on an adventure.

"Where shall we start?" she asked Max.

"I thought we'd start with the public rooms."

"Public rooms?"

"Yes, those are the rooms where the royal family entertains."

"I'm intrigued. Lead the way."

She pushed aside thoughts of dining with his mother. At least, she tried to push the worries aside. Still, it was difficult. She'd never had anyone instantly dislike her. She tried hard to get along with everyone. Maybe she hadn't tried hard enough with his mother. Yes, that was it. She would try harder.

"Is something bothering you?" Max's voice jarred her from her thoughts as they descended the grand staircase.

"Why?"

"You're quieter than normal."

"Sorry." She glanced around the grand foyer. It was spacious enough to have a formal ball right here. "I can't believe this place is so big."

"It's great for playing hide-and-seek."

"Really?" She turned to him, finding a serious look on his face. "You really played in here."

He nodded. "When we were young, my brother and I could spend hours playing hide-and-seek. Why do you seem so surprised?"

"Because this is a palace." She glanced over at the oriental vase beneath a large mirror. "Everything in here is breakable and must cost a fortune. It's more like a museum than a playground."

He smiled. "Maybe to you. To my brother and me, it was home."

"Was home?"

Max shrugged. "I guess I've been away from

here longer than I thought." He pointed to the left. "Shall we go this way?"

She gazed up at the priceless artwork on the walls. "Sounds good to me. This place is absolutely amazing."

Max chuckled. "My mother would approve."

So she needed to compliment his mother. Noemi tucked away this nugget of information. They toured a lot of the rooms on the main floor, including a red room with portraits of Max's ancestors. Some of the paintings were very old. The outfits they wore were quite elaborate, both for the men and the women.

And then Noemi came across a portrait of a baby in a christening gown. It was the eyes that drew her in. They looked so familiar. "Is that you?"

"Yes. One day it will be replaced by a formal portrait after the coronation with my crown, scepter and cape."

It drove home his importance and how Max was so not like any of the other men that she'd ever dated. One day he would rule Ostania. She couldn't even imagine what it would be like to carry such an enormous responsibility. And here she was struggling with the demands of caring for one baby whereas he would be responsible for millions of lives.

As she continued to stare at Max's baby picture, she wondered if that was how their baby would look. Would it be a boy and the image of his father? Or would it be a girl?

Noemi glanced around the room to make sure they were alone and then lowered her voice. "Do you want a son? Or a daughter?"

Max's eyes momentarily widened. When he spoke, it was in a hushed tone. "To be honest, I hadn't given that much thought. Just finding out that I'm going to be a father has been quite a shock."

"But if you had to choose, would you want a son or a daughter?"

Max looked as though he were giving the question some serious thought. "Would you be upset if I say I don't care as long as it's healthy?"

She smiled. "No. I like that answer. I feel the same. I will love this baby no matter what."

"Me, too."

"The thing worrying me is that I don't have a clue what I'm doing. So I bought some baby books. They tell me what to expect at the different stages."

"Maybe you should loan me those books when you're done."

Her gaze met his. "You'd really read them?"

"Of course I would. I keep telling you, we're in this together."

"You don't know how much I want to believe you." And then she realized she'd vocalized her thoughts.

His head lowered to hers. Ever so softly, he said, "Then believe this."

He pressed his lips to hers. In that moment, she knew how deeply she'd missed his touch. As his lips moved over hers, she couldn't remember the reason she'd been holding him at arm's length. She was certain it must have made sense at one point but not any longer.

Her hands rested against his chest—his very firm, very muscular chest. His kiss teased and tempted her. As a moan built in the back of her throat, she slipped her arms over his shoulders and leaned her body into his.

Knock. Knock.

And then someone cleared their throat.

Noemi jumped out of Max's arms. Heat scorched her cheeks. *Please don't let it be the queen.*

"Yes, Sloan," Max said.

"Your Highness, I was sent to let you know that dinner will be served in fifteen minutes."

"Thank you."

And with that the butler turned and disappeared down the hallway.

Noemi wasn't sure how to react. When she turned back to Max, he was quietly chuckling. She frowned. "I don't know what you find so amusing."

He sobered up. "Absolutely nothing." His eyes still twinkled with amusement. "Shall we continue the tour?"

"Are there more rooms on this floor to see?"

Max nodded. He led her down the hallway to the throne room with two massive chairs with carved wood backs and red cushions. Behind the chairs was the family's coat of arms. And then there was a library, but not just any library. The room was enormous. The bookcases soared so high on the wall that there was a ladder to reach the upper shelves.

"Do you think your family would mind if I borrowed a book or two while I'm here?" She liked to read at night. It relaxed her and was something she looked forward to in the evenings. "I was in such a rush to get packed that I didn't think to grab any of mine."

"Help yourself. This room doesn't get utilized as much as it should." He glanced at the gold clock on the console behind one of the couches.

"Shall we head into dinner? I can show you the rest of palace later or perhaps tomorrow."

"Yes, let's go." The last thing she wanted was to upset his mother by being late for dinner.

"That hungry?"

"Something like that." Right now, food was the last thing on her mind.

Max stepped in front of her. "Before we go, I want to reassure you that I have not forgotten about your doctor's appointment. In the morning, we can make some phone calls and if worst comes to worst, I'll fly you back to Mont Coeur for the day."

"You really would, wouldn't you?"

"I'd do anything for my family."

Before she could say a word, he kissed her. It was just a brief kiss but enough to make her heart skip a beat.

As Max took her arm to lead her into the dining room, he leaned in close to her ear. "Don't worry. Once my mother gets to know you, she's going to really like you."

"I hope you're right." Though Noemi doubted it, that didn't mean she wouldn't try to make a good impression.

His parents and brother were already at the other end of the long narrow room. The dining table was bigger than any she'd ever seen. It could easily seat two dozen people.

Noemi leaned close to Max, catching a whiff of his spicy cologne. For a moment, she forgot what she was about to say. All she could think about was Max and how easy it would be to turn into his arms and kiss him again.

"Noemi?" Max sent her a puzzled look. "Are you all right?"

"Um, yes."

He guided her across the room. The family stopped talking and turned to them. Noemi's stomach shivered with nerves. Her gaze met the king's. He sent her a warm smile. The queen didn't smile but she didn't frown either. Noemi chose to count that as a positive sign.

"So you're my brother's girlfriend?" Tobias asked.

Noemi's gaze moved to Max's younger brother. He had blondish-brown hair like his brother. Tobias was an inch or so shorter than Max. But he wasn't as reserved as Max. In fact, he was free with a smile that made his eyes twinkle. He wasn't as handsome as Max but he'd be a close second.

He took her hand in his and kissed the back with a fluttery kiss. She was so caught off guard that she didn't have time to react. It took a moment for her to realize her mouth was slightly agape. She quickly pressed her lips together.

"It's so nice to meet you, Prince Tobias." And then because she wasn't sure how to greet him, she did a slight curtsy and dipped her head.

When she straightened, Prince Tobias shook his head. "Relax. It's only us here. Please tell me my brother doesn't make you curtsy to him."

Max cleared his throat. "That's enough, Tobias."

"That's right, Tobias," the queen spoke up. "Please remember your manners."

Noemi wasn't sure if the queen was coming to her defense or if the queen didn't like the lack of proper etiquette.

The queen turned to her. "I hope you found your room adequate."

"It's quite lovely." *Lovely? Really? That's the best you can do.* "Thank you so much for having me. Max—erm, the prince has shown me around the palace and it is breathtaking. I especially love the library."

The queen's eyes widened. "You read?"

Noemi smiled and nodded. She was at last making some headway with the queen. "I read every chance I get." Not wanting to let go of this first legitimate connection with the queen, Noemi said, "I find biographies fascinating. And I enjoy historical accounts."

Before the queen could say more, dinner was announced and everyone moved to the table. Noemi was relieved to see that they were all seated at one end of the table. She didn't want to have to shout the entire length of the table in order to make dinner conversation.

Max hadn't warned her that dinner would be quite so lengthy. It had six courses and it was not rushed. The family for the most part was like any other with each person catching the others up on what was going on in their lives. However, they were more reserved than her family as there was no joking, teasing or laughing. Still, the meal was more relaxed than she'd been expecting.

And so she made her way through the whole evening without any problems with the queen. Maybe the need to rush back to Mont Coeur wasn't necessary after all. She really was curious to learn more about Max's home.

Noemi turned her attention to Max as he discussed the possibility of purchasing a new horse with the king. And her other reason for wanting to stay might have to do with those kisses he'd laid on her. What did they mean? And where would they lead them?

CHAPTER TWELVE

PERHAPS HE'D BEEN hoping for too much—too soon.

The next morning, Max had been summoned to a cabinet meeting to bring him up to speed on everything he'd missed during his time away. The only problem was his mind kept straying to Noemi.

Though dinner the prior evening had gone without a hitch, it had still been reserved with Noemi left out of most of the conversation. He hadn't realized until then just how important his family's acceptance of Noemi was to him. But what was even more important was Noemi feeling comfortable around not only him but also his family. How else would she consider raising their child as an Ostanian?

All was not lost yet. He still had a chance to win her over. And if she felt up to it, he planned to show her some of the charms of Ostania.

"I have to go," he told his mother and father, as well as the royal advisors. He'd promised

Noemi that they'd sort out her doctor's appointment.

"Go? Go where?" his father asked.

"This is important," his mother chimed in. "You can't just disregard your royal duties. I know that we've given you a lot a leeway—"

"Perhaps more than we should have," his father finished his mother's sentence. "It is time you quit chasing women and partying. It's time you take your position in this family seriously. You may not end up as king, but that doesn't mean you won't have an important role to fill."

Max noticed his father didn't look quite right. His complexion was paler than at dinner the prior evening and there were dark circles under his eyes. Max couldn't help wondering how long his father had looked this way. Things had definitely changed in the time he'd been away. It appeared that he'd been gone too long.

"I understand," Max said. "I will do more. But right now, I have a guest."

"Right now, you have work to do," the queen insisted. "Your guest can wait."

His mother was right. He needed to do more to alleviate some of the burden from his father's shoulders. And to be honest, Noemi with her morning sickness wasn't up for much until her stomach settled. He checked the time. He had at least another hour before she'd want to go out. They could arrange for the doctor's appointment before they left the palace.

"Just let me make a phone call." Then on second thought, he didn't want his family to overhear his conversation. He settled for jotting out a note and sending it with one of the staff. He didn't want Noemi to think he'd forgotten her.

Noemi smiled.

For the first time in a while, she didn't feel like utter rubbish. Now that she was settling into her second trimester, the doctor said the morning sickness should start to abate. Apparently her doctor had been correct. *Thank goodness.*

She'd actually slept well and had some energy. She couldn't wait to go explore Ostania. So when there was a knock at the door, she rushed over and opened it with a smile. The smile slipped from her face when she realized it wasn't Max.

A man in a dark uniform handed her a white folded paper. "This is from His Royal Highness Prince Maximilian."

She accepted the paper. "Thank you."

With a curt nod, the man took a step back. He turned and headed down the hall. She wondered why Max was sending her a note instead of showing up in person. She hoped that nothing was wrong.

Apologies.
Unavoidably delayed. Will catch up with you ASAP. Feel free to make use of the library.
Max

She was disappointed he couldn't join her. She realized she'd been missing him more than she probably should. In fact, he'd been on her mind since the prior evening when he'd escorted her back to her room after his family had coffee. She'd been hoping for another kiss but it hadn't happened.

She wondered if all the royal dinners took close to two hours. Or was it something special because she was there? Then she realized it was more than likely due to Max's return.

Either way, it had gone far better than she ever imagined that it would. Max was charming. His brother was entertaining, almost comical at times. His mother, though still reserved, was more cordial and even gave her some reading suggestions regarding the history of Ostania. And though the king was far quieter at dinner than he had been when she'd first met him, all in all it had been a good evening. Maybe the royals weren't all that different after all.

Max's invitation to explore the library more fully was an invitation that she couldn't pass up. Bundled in a bulky sweater—without being situated near a roaring fire, the palace was a bit on the chilly side—Noemi made her way to the library without getting lost. But even if she had, there was so much staff around that someone would have pointed her in the right direction.

When she reached the library, the sun was poking through the stained-glass windows, sending a kaleidoscope of colors throughout the room. She didn't know the room with its floor-to-ceiling shelves could look any more appealing, but the touch of color made it seem…well, magical.

She moved to the closest shelf and started reading the titles. When she found one that intrigued her, she pulled it out to examine more closely. It wasn't until she strayed across a book the queen had recommended that she was hooked. Noemi knew the book wouldn't include Max but it would be about his ancestors and her baby's ancestors. She wanted to know as much as she could.

She carried the book back to her room to read while waiting for Max. She moved to a couch near one of the windows and settled in. The more she learned of Max and his life here in Ostania, the more she wanted to know about the country. She opened the leather-bound book and started to read. However, every couple of minutes her gaze moved to the doorway. How much longer would he be?

As chapter one turned to chapter two, then three, she had to wonder what was keeping him. He hadn't hinted about the cause of his delay in the note. Had something happened? Had he changed his mind about spending the day with her? Had he realized that she didn't fit in here?

As though he sensed her worries, Max appeared in the doorway. She immediately closed the book and got to her feet. She smiled but he didn't return the gesture.

She approached him. "What's wrong?"

"Why should there be something wrong?"

She shrugged. "I…um…it's just that you look like you have something on your mind. If it's me—"

"It's not. Don't ever think that." He paused as

though gathering his thoughts. "I'm just sorry for being late. I hope you didn't get bored."

"Actually, I found this very informative book about the history of Ostania. Do you think anyone would mind if I keep it here until I finish reading it?"

He shook his head. "Please borrow whatever books appeal to you."

She placed the book on her nightstand. "I think just this one for now."

"To make up for being late, I have a surprise for you."

It was then that she noticed he was holding his arms behind his back. "Did I tell you that I love surprises? I always hoped my parents would throw me a surprise party with all my friends from school."

"I take it they didn't?"

She shook her head. "They were always too busy with the company."

"Would you like me to throw you a party?"

She studied him for a moment. "You're serious, aren't you?"

"Is there any reason I shouldn't be?"

She smiled at him and shook her head. "I'm past the age of longing for a surprise party, but I think I'll do one for our son or daughter. What do you think?"

"As long as you include cake, balloons and a pony, they'll love it."

Her smile broadened as they talked of their child's future. "I think the only thing that will capture their attention will be the pony."

"You might be right." A serious look came over his face. "Will you continue to work after the baby's born?"

"I'd like to." She'd been rolling this around in her mind for some time. "But I plan to step down as the face of Cattaneo Jewels."

"Really?" His eyes reflected his surprise.

She nodded. "I've been thinking about this for a while."

"What will you do? Take another role within your family's business?"

She shook her head. "I don't want to work with my brother. He...he doesn't take my opinions seriously."

"You have plenty of other career choices."

"I'd like it to be something meaningful like... like head up a foundation...or champion a worthy cause."

"I'm sure whatever you settle on will definitely benefit from your attention."

"I hope you're right." Her gaze moved to his arm that was still behind his back. "So what's my surprise?"

"Are you sure you still want it?" He sent her a teasing smile. "Are you sure you're not too old for a surprise?"

"I'll never be that old." She reached for his arm, but he stepped back out of her reach. "Show me."

He was still smiling. "After this big buildup, I hope you aren't disappointed with them—"

"There's more than one?"

He nodded and then he held out the purple lion and the white booties.

"You got them?" She accepted the gifts. "But how?"

"I have my ways. And I knew how important they were to you."

In that moment, Max left a definite impression on her. No one had ever done something so thoughtful for her. Her eyes grew misty. *Stupid hormones.*

"Thank you."

"You're welcome." He closed her bedroom door. "Are you ready to make some very important phone calls?"

The doctor's appointment. "Yes, I am."

She talked to her doctor in Mont Coeur and then Max spoke with a local doctor he said could be trusted. In the end, the sonogram would be done in Ostania two days from now.

It was arranged for after office hours to aid their privacy.

"Now that that is all settled, would you like to go visit the village?"

"I would." Already dressed in a bulky sweater and her black tights, she was ready to go exploring.

Lucky for her, she'd remembered her black knee-high boots along with her long-sleeve black hooded coat with gray faux fur trim. And so a few minutes later, she was settled in the passenger seat while Max sat behind the steering wheel.

"I didn't know you knew how to drive," she said, surprised to find him so at ease behind the wheel.

"The security staff doesn't like when I drive, but I don't like being escorted everywhere I go."

She glanced in the side mirror. "Isn't that your bodyguards behind us?"

"Yes, but at least I have a little distance from them. I can talk on the phone without being overheard or I can turn up the stereo as loud as I want without them frowning."

"So you aren't a perfect prince after all?"

"Perfect prince?" He laughed. "You do remember how we met, don't you?"

"Oh, I remember." She lightly patted her belly. "I'll never forget it."

For a while they road in a comfortable silence. She hadn't seen this playful side of Max since they'd arrived in Ostania. He always looked as though he was carrying around a great weight. She didn't realize until that moment how much she'd missed this part of him—the dreamy smile on his face—the way his eyes sparkled when he teased her. Maybe today would be more entertaining than she ever imagined.

"What are you thinking?" Max asked.

"What makes you think I have something on my mind?"

"Because you have that devilish look in your eyes."

"Devilish look? No one has ever accused me of that before." She leaned her head back on the seat as a smile played on her lips. This was the best she'd felt in a very long time. "Why, Prince Max, is this your attempt to flirt with me?"

Max maneuvered the small car into a streetside parking spot. He cut the engine and then turned to her. He rested an arm over the top of her seat. "I don't know. Is it working?"

With his face so close, her heart started to pound. "Do you remember what happened the last time you flirted with me?"

"I do." His face was so close now that his breath tickled her cheek. "In fact, I can't forget it. You've ruined me for any other woman."

She knew he was just having fun with her, but it didn't stop her from lowering her gaze to his lips. The truth was she hadn't been able to forget about their night together either or her desire for a repeat. It filled her dreams at night and tantalizing images swooped in during the day, stealing her train of thought. The way he kissed her made her feel like she was the only woman in the world. And when his fingers stroked her cheek, as they were doing now, her heart skipped a beat.

She leaned toward him as he gravitated toward her. They met in the middle. There was no hesitation. Both kissed as though they needed the connection as much as they needed oxygen.

His lips pressed hard against hers. She opened her mouth to him and their tongues met. Her pulse quickened. Her hand reached out to him, wrapping around the back of his neck and stroking up through his thick hair.

Mm… Each kiss was better than the last. She released the seat belt, wanting to get closer to him. If only they weren't in a car—

Tap. Tap.

Noemi jerked back. Her eyes opened and

glanced around, finding the men in dark suits on either side of Max's car.

"Sorry they startled you." Max settled back in his seat. "It's their protocol when we're in public. They were letting me know that the vicinity is safe for me to exit the car."

"Oh. I felt like a teenager getting busted making out in the car."

He smiled playfully. "So you were that kind of girl?"

"Hey." She lightly smacked him on the shoulder. "I didn't say I did it. I said... Oh, never mind. I shouldn't have said anything."

"Yes, you should. I like learning these things about you."

"Really?" Somehow it just struck her as surprising that a royal prince would be interested in her rather boring life.

He nodded. "Why wouldn't I be? I find you fascinating."

"You're the fascinating one. A prince who escapes the confines of the palace to live a wild partying lifestyle."

"Maybe. Maybe not."

"Maybe not?" He'd piqued her curiosity. "What aren't you telling me?"

Max hesitated. "Never mind. We should go explore the Christmas market."

And with that he alighted from the car. She joined him on the side of the road. Without a word, he reached for her hand. With the sun out, it warmed the air ever so slightly, making it unnecessary for gloves. His fingers wrapped around hers.

She knew she should pull away, but she didn't want to. It felt right to have her fingers entwined with his. The more time they spent together, the more it seemed as though this was how they were meant to be—together.

She glanced up at him. "Aren't you worried about the press?"

He shrugged. "This is Ostania. And more so this is Vallée Verte. These people have known me all my life. They are, shall we say, protective. So when the press comes sniffing around, they make sure they are not welcome. As a result, the press doesn't come here much."

She could see why the townspeople would feel an allegiance to Max. He was kind and thoughtful to everyone, even those he didn't know.

And so they strolled through the village and had a leisurely lunch at a bistro with a hot cup of soup and a warm sandwich. Noemi's appetite kept growing and so did her waistline. It was one of the reasons for the sonogram a few weeks early.

After lunch, they strolled to the Christmas market. Noemi found something to buy for each of her family members. This Christmas was so important. It was the first without their parents and it was the first with Leo. She desperately wanted her brothers to come together, but she feared control of the family business would drive a permanent wedge between them. And she would never have a close family—like she used to know.

Her gaze moved to Max as he checked out some Christmas ornaments. Technically he would be her family, too. The baby would form a lifetime connection between them. But what would that look like?

In that moment, a little girl bumped into her.

"Hi there," Noemi said.

The girl must have been about four or five. She peered up at Noemi with tears in her eyes. Noemi looked around for the girl's parents but no one appeared to be with her.

The girl started to move away.

Noemi ran after her. She stepped in the girl's path. "Where is your mommy?"

The girl's gaze frantically searched the market. "I… I don't know."

Noemi felt bad for her. She glanced around for Max, but he was some ways away with his back to them. She couldn't just let the little girl run off alone—not even in Vallée Verte.

Noemi knelt down. "Can I help you find your parents?"

The little girl shrugged. Tears in her big brown eyes splashed onto her chubby cheeks.

"My name's Noemi. What's yours?"

"Gemma."

"Well, Gemma, it's nice to meet you." She didn't have much experience with children. She supposed she'd better learn quickly, seeing as in just a handful of months, she'd be a mother. "Come with me." She held out her hand.

The little girl hesitated.

She couldn't blame her. She didn't know Noemi at all. "I promise I won't hurt you. I just want to help you find your parents."

The little girl slipped her cold hand in hers.

"Do you have gloves?"

Gemma shrugged.

Noemi spied a bit of white sticking out of the pockets of the little girl's bright red jacket. "There they are."

She helped Gemma put on her gloves.

"I'm hungry," the little girl whined. And by the looks of her, probably tired, too.

"Okay." Noemi glanced around. There were a lot of food booths in the Christmas market. "We'll get you some food first and then find your parents. They have to be around here."

As Noemi made her way toward Max, she asked the vendors if they knew the girl. None of them did. The parents had to be frantic. But where were they? If this was her baby, she'd be standing on a table, yelling so everyone could hear her.

"Noemi?" Max's gaze moved from her to the little girl. "Who is this?"

"Max, meet Gemma. She is lost. We're trying to find her parents." Noemi noticed that he had some food in his hand. "Are you going to eat that?"

He glanced down at the pastry. "You can have it."

Though it did look tempting, she said, "It's for Gemma. She's hungry."

Max knelt down. "Would you like this?"

The girl hesitated but eventually accepted the pastry. She took a bite. Then another.

While Gemma enjoyed the food, Max turned to Noemi. "We'll give her to one of my security men. They'll make sure the authorities find her family."

Gemma tightened her hold on Noemi's leg. The girl looked up at her with pleading eyes.

Noemi's protective instinct kicked in. "Can't she stay with us? You know, until we find her parents?"

Max's brows furrowed together. "Noemi, how do you expect to find them?"

She'd been giving this some thought. Her gaze met Max's. "I have an idea but I'll need your help."

"What do you want me to do?"

"Can you lift Gemma onto your shoulders?" When he nodded, Noemi knelt down next to Gemma. "The prince is going to pick you up so you can look over the crowd for your parents. Is that all right?"

Gemma cupped a hand to her mouth. "He's the prince?"

Noemi smiled and nodded. "He is. Can he pick you up?"

The girl sent Max a hesitant stare and then shook her head. The girl clutched Noemi's leg. Noemi's heart went out to her. She couldn't imagine how scared the girl must be.

Noemi smoothed a hand over the girl's head. "It's okay. We're just trying to help you."

Gemma glanced at Max again, but she didn't release Noemi's leg.

Noemi mouthed to Max, *Say something*.

Max sent her was puzzled look. He mouthed, *What?*

She mouthed back, *Anything*.

Max cleared his throat. Who would have guessed Max would be nervous around a child? She wondered if he would be that nervous with their baby.

Max knelt down next to the girl. "Hi. My name's Max. Would you like to be friends?"

Gemma shrugged, keeping a firm hold on Noemi's leg.

Noemi intervened. "Gemma, he's a really good friend of mine. You can trust him. I promise." When Gemma didn't lessen her hold, Noemi continued, "And I'll be right here with you the whole time. He'll just pick you up for a moment to look for your parents. And then he'll put you back down." She paused a moment to give the little girl a chance to think about it. "You do want to find your parents, don't you?"

Gemma slowly nodded.

With Max kneeling, he held out his arms to Gemma. The girl let him lift her.

This interaction made Noemi eager to meet her own child. She wondered if it would be a girl or boy. Should she find out soon? Her gaze moved back to Max, trying to imagine him with their child.

"Do you see them?" Max asked.

Gemma shook her head and then she reached her arms out to Noemi. The girl was so sweet. The parents must be so worried. Noemi took the girl in her arms.

Max leaned over to Noemi. "Don't worry. We'll make sure she gets back to her parents."

It was then that Noemi noticed the policeman approaching them. He must have been patrolling the area when one of Max's guards flagged him down. She wasn't the only one to notice the man's approach. The girl's arms tightened around Noemi's neck.

"It's okay," she said to Gemma. Then she turned to Max. "I can't hand her over. She's already scared enough."

"They are better equipped to handle this." Max pleaded with his eyes. "Noemi, this is for the best."

Max turned to speak with the officer, explaining the situation. The officer assured Max that he would return the child to her family. The officer moved to Noemi and reached for Gemma.

"No…" Gemma tightened her grip to the point where it was uncomfortable for Noemi.

"Stop." Noemi stared at the officer. There had to be a better way to do this. Then her gaze strayed across the concerned look on Max's face. "Just give me a moment."

"Noemi..." Max frowned at her.

"Just wait." She rapidly searched her mind for the best way to reunite this little girl with her parents.

The policeman stepped away and spoke into his radio.

Noemi's gaze searched the market. There were a number of people in this part of the market, but none appeared to be looking for a lost little girl. A band playing folksy music was situated in the center while food vendors and artists had tents along the edges of the market area where they displayed their goods.

Noemi got another idea and took off.

"Noemi, where are you going?"

She waved at Max to follow her. She rushed over to the band that was on a little stand. When the band members noticed the prince approaching, they stopped mid-piece. With a flustered look, they got to their feet and bowed their heads at the prince.

Max greeted them and told them what a marvelous job they were doing. And then Noemi asked them for a favor. The four older men were more than happy to accommodate her.

With Max and Gemma next to her, Noemi stepped up to the microphone. "Excuse me."

Most of the crowd wasn't paying attention. Noemi placed her fingers between her lips and blew. The high-pitched whistle brought silence over the marketplace. Everyone turned her way.

"I'm sorry to disturb your afternoon but we have a bit of a situation. This little girl has been separated from her parents, are they here?" She scanned the crowd, searching for frantic parents to come rushing toward the stage.

There was no movement. No frantic parents.

And then she had another thought. "Please help me reunite the little girl with her parents. Everyone who has a cell phone, please pull it out. If you all start texting on your social media accounts, hopefully word will make it to Gemma's parents. Use #HelpGemma. Thank you."

When no one moved, Noemi turned to Max. She whispered, "You do have cell phones in Ostania, don't you?"

Max laughed, a deep rich sound that warmed her insides. "Yes, *ma chérie*. We have cell phones and the internet."

Noemi sighed. "Thank goodness." She glanced

at the people who were still motionless and staring at them. "Why aren't they doing anything?"

Max looked at her. "Excuse me." When she stepped aside, he moved to the microphone. "Please, help."

All it took was two words from Max in order to spur people into motion. She glanced at him and sent him a small smile—a hopeful smile. This was going to work. It had to work—for Gemma's sake.

Max moved away from the microphone. "Now what?"

"We wait. We'll browse the Christmas market and maybe get some more to eat." She turned to Gemma. "Would you like that?"

Gemma nodded.

And then Noemi added, "Your parents will find us. Just wait and see."

Max sent her a reassuring smile.

She set Gemma on the ground and took her small hand in her own. Then Noemi turned to Max. "Why do you keep looking at me like that?"

"Because I've never seen this side of you."

"What side?"

"The assertive, take-charge mode. You are quite impressive. And you think fast on your toes. You would make a good leader."

"Leader?" She couldn't help but smile. Not letting his words go to her head, she said, "I'm helping a lost child. Nothing more."

"I think you're capable of far more than you give yourself credit for."

She didn't even know if she would make a good mother. She had so much to learn and no parents to turn to for advice. A rush of pregnancy hormones hit her. Doubts about her ability to be a good mother assailed her. What if she messed up her kid? What if she was the worst mother ever?

"Hey, relax." A concerned look came over Max's face. Apparently, her worries were reflected on her face. Max placed a reassuring hand on her shoulder. "I didn't mean to upset you. I was just trying to help."

Noemi shook her head. "It's not you."

"Then what is it?"

She shook her head. "Nothing."

But inside she was a ball of nerves. She didn't even know what she was going to do for a job if she walked away from modeling. Sebastian had made it clear she wasn't welcome in the family business except as a silent partner. She recalled how her parents were hard on him while growing up and how he'd done his best to shield her.

Noemi wondered if that's what he thought

he was still doing—protecting her. Sometimes habits were hard to break. And now with Leo joining the company, she would definitely be in the way.

Her whole future was one big question mark.

CHAPTER THIRTEEN

MAX GLANCED OVER at Noemi with her hand wrapped around Gemma's. They'd stopped at a stand where handmade toys were displayed. He was captivated with the way Noemi's face lit up as she talked to the little girl.

He could so easily imagine her with their own child. And after witnessing her strong protective instincts today and her caring way with Gemma, he had no doubt Noemi would make a remarkable mother.

"Shall we eat?" Max asked. He'd spotted a stand where they offered a variety of food that didn't involve sugar.

Gemma turned to Noemi as though trying to decide if she should agree or not. When Noemi agreed, Gemma smiled and nodded her head.

It was remarkable how the little girl had taken to Noemi so quickly. But then again, he'd been drawn to Noemi from across the room without having spoken one word to her. And it went beyond her outward beauty. There was something in her smile and a genuine kindness in the way she dealt with people. Everyone around her seemed to enjoy her company. Even his mother was beginning to thaw around Noemi. And that was saying a lot.

After the food had been presented, the vendor refused to take Max's money. This wasn't the first time something like this had happened. And though Max was touched by the offer, he knew these people couldn't afford to freely give away their goods—nor should they be expected to. And so he mentioned to his bodyguard to make a note of their names and then they would be generously compensated later.

As the three of them ate their selection of croissants and meats while sitting on a bench off to the side of the market, Max noticed that Noemi was busy on her phone. He wondered what had her so preoccupied that she'd barely eaten any of her food. But then he noticed she was following the hashtag for Gemma.

"Relax. We'll find her parents."

Noemi slipped the phone back in her purse. "Don't make promises you can't keep."

"This is one promise I intend to keep."

The urge to lean over and give Noemi a reassuring kiss came over him. It was so strong that he started in her direction before he caught himself. This wasn't the place for a public display of affection. Suddenly he was anxious to head back to the privacy of the palace.

"I'm sorry," Noemi said.

Lost in his thoughts, he wasn't sure what she was referring to. "Sorry for what?"

"I'm sure you have more important things to do than sit here with us."

The truth was that he did have a meeting with the royal cabinet. They wanted to discuss options to pump up a sluggish economy. At first, the subject hadn't interested him. It had sounded dry and boring. But after spending this time in the village with the very kind and generous residents, he was anxious to do what he could to improve their lives.

However, he wouldn't just leave Noemi to deal with Gemma. He could already sense the strong bond forming between the two. If the police tried to remove the child before the parents were found, he knew there would be a scene. And he didn't want that for Noemi or Gemma.

"I have nothing more important than being here with you." Did that sound as strange to her as it did to him? He never talked that way.

Noemi rewarded him with a smile. "Thank

you. I'm certain Gemma's parents will turn up soon."

And then there was a commotion off to the side of market. Both of Max's bodyguards and the police officers stood between him and the commotion. The excited voices were getting louder as though approaching them. Max's body stiffened.

Once as a child, his family had come under attack from an angry and disillusioned person. They had blamed the king for all their personal problems and had tried to harm the royal family. Since then, loud commotions in public spots put Max on guard.

He got to his feet and motioned for Noemi and Gemma to remain where they were. When he spoke to his guard, the man said he didn't know what was going on.

Max was about to call in additional security for Noemi when a man and woman appeared in front of the police. The woman had tears in her eyes and the man was speaking so quickly that it was hard to catch what he was saying.

And then Gemma rushed forward. "Mama! Mama!"

That was all the confirmation Max needed to move aside and let the girl by. Gemma rushed into her mother's arms.

In the end, it came to light that Gemma had been anxious to see the Christmas market, but her parents had some shopping to do first at the local shops on the other side of the village. Gemma had slipped away to visit the market, but then couldn't remember how to get back to her parents. Gemma had learned a valuable lesson and had promised her parents never to do something like that again.

"Thank you so much," Gemma's father said to Prince Max.

"It's not me you should thank." Max turned to Noemi. "She was the one that thought of using social media to locate you and reunite you with your daughter."

With a watery smile, the mother profusely thanked Noemi. And though Noemi looked uncomfortable with all the attention, she accepted the kind words graciously.

And then out of nowhere Gemma pulled away from her mother and gave Noemi a big hug. Noemi asked if they could have their picture taken together. When Gemma and her parents agreed, Max pulled out his phone. He noticed that he had three missed calls on his phone. His absence had not gone unnoticed. This trip into the village had taken much longer than he'd imagined. He dismissed his thoughts of what would face him back at the palace and used his cell phone to snap a picture, promising to forward it to Noemi.

Max's bodyguard, Roc, stepped up next to him and spoke softly near his ear. "You are needed at the palace right away. It's an emergency."

That word was never thrown around lightly. The hairs on the back of his neck raised. Max nodded and then waited until there was a pause in the conversation between Noemi and Gemma's parents.

"Noemi, I must go back to the palace."

Noemi's smile faded. "We were just going to finish touring the remaining shops."

He felt bad that their day had been interrupted. He lifted his phone and checked his missed phone calls. To his surprise, only one was from the royal cabinet and the other two were from his mother. His mother didn't make a phone call unless it was important. The emergency must be personal. His father?

None of this concerned Noemi and she wouldn't have anything to do back at the palace while he was dealing with his mother. He wanted this trip to be enjoyable for her. And so far, it hadn't gone quite as he'd planned.

"Why don't you stay here and finish touring

the village?" he said to Noemi before he leaned over to his bodyguards and instructed one of them to stay with her.

"Really? You don't mind?" Noemi looked unsure about the idea.

"Not at all." Liar. He did mind. He longed to spend more time with her. "I'll meet you later for dinner."

"It's a date."

He liked the sound of a date. It gave him something good to look forward to. "Roc will be staying with you and escorting you back to the palace."

"But that's not necessary—"

"It's nonnegotiable." The lift of her brows told him he'd misspoken. He'd never felt so protective of another person. The rush of emotion had him coming across too strongly, "I just want to make sure you don't get lost or anything."

Her face took on a neutral tone. The smile on her face returned. "I don't think that will happen. It's a little hard to miss the palace on the hill. It kind of stands out."

He smiled, too. "I guess you have a point, but this way you'll have a ride back whenever you're ready to go. It's a long walk. Trust me. I know from experience."

"Thank you. That would be nice."

He definitely had to make sure to take a lighter approach when the protective instinct came over him. "You're welcome."

She had no idea how much he wanted to stay there with her. He didn't care what they toured, he just wanted to be around her and bask in the glow of her smile and listen to the musical sound of her laughter. He was hooked on Noemi. And it was a dangerous place to be should she decide life in Ostania wasn't for her—he couldn't leave now or ever again. He had to prepare to rule a nation.

Back at the palace, the bright cheery decorations seemed to mock him.

Max was torn between duty to family and duty to nation. On top of it, he was greatly concerned about this emergency. The butler instructed him to go upstairs. It was his father and the doctor had been called.

Max rushed to his father's bedchamber. He'd stayed away for too long. He'd made his father carry the brunt of the weight of caring for a nation all on his own and it had been too much for him.

His mother stopped him in the hallway. "Maximilian, slow down."

"But Father…how is he?"

"The doctor is in with him." His mother didn't say it but she was very worried.

"What happened?"

His mother gazed up at him. In that moment, it was as though she'd aged twenty years. "It's your father's diabetes, there've been complications. His kidneys—they aren't functioning well."

Max raked his fingers through his hair. He knew about his father's diabetes. His father had had it most of his life, but it had always been under control—until recent years. But Max had no idea it was this bad. "Why is this the first I'm hearing of it?"

His mother frowned at him. "Because your father refused to let anyone tell you. He said you needed time to recover from those years of dealing with…with your illness." His mother never could bring herself to say the word cancer. "Your father said everything would be all right and there was no reason to worry you or your brother. But over time, it's getting worse."

"So Tobias doesn't know either?"

With tears shimmering in his mother's eyes, she shook her head.

The door to the bedroom opened and the doctor exited. Max stepped up next to his mother.

He had so many questions. He needed to know just how serious this situation was and what he could do to make it better.

The doctor held up a hand to him. "The king just wants the queen right now. Please wait here."

In this instance, the doctor trumped royalty. His mother disappeared into the room and the door closed. Max was left alone—on the outside, looking in. His head started to pound as question after question came to him. How did he let himself become this disconnected with his family?

He had to do better. How was he ever going to make a good father when he couldn't even stay on top of the family members he already had?

He turned around to start pacing when he noticed his brother sitting at the far end of the hallway. Tobias was sitting with his head in his hands.

Max approached him. He took a seat and searched for something comforting to say. It wasn't easy when he was as worried as his brother looked. "Hey, it's going to be okay."

Tobias shook his head. "No, it isn't."

"Do you know something I don't?" Considering Max didn't know much at this point, it was quite possible.

Tobias ran his forearm over his face. "They've been talking about Father stepping down."

"From the throne?" Max never imagined his father would ever agree to such a thing.

Tobias nodded. "I... I can't do it."

"Sure you can."

Tobias's eyes were wide with worry. "No, I can't. This should be you. You should be taking over."

Max searched for the right words to comfort his brother. "You're just worried. Everything will seem clearer tomorrow."

Tobias shook his head. "I don't know why they make such a big deal of having an heir. Look at you. You're calm. You can handle this stuff."

Max raked his fingers through his hair. "They've been working with you. You know how to run the country."

Tobias got to his feet. "I don't want to!"

Max stood. He placed his hands on his brother's shoulders. "Okay. Calm down."

"How am I supposed to do that? Our father is sick. Very sick. I'm too young for all of this. I... I'm not the right person."

Max knew how to comfort his brother. But

was it the right time to mention the baby? Things with Noemi were still unsettled.

But he never imagined his father's health would have declined this drastically. Max's gaze searched his brother's bloodshot eyes. He'd never seen his brother so scared. Not since Max had cancer. It was so wrong for his brother to be this upset when he could help alleviate some of his worry.

"Tobias, you can stop worrying about shouldering Papa's responsibilities."

"What?" Tobias's gaze searched his. "Of course I can't. You know this. I'm the spare heir."

"Tobias, listen to me." Max glanced around to make sure they were alone. Then he turned back to his brother. "I have something I need to tell you."

Tobias turned to him. "If it's bad, now isn't the time."

The thought of his baby brought a smile to Max's face. "It's not bad. In fact, it's good news. Really, really good news."

"Well, don't just stand there. Share."

"You can't tell anyone this. Okay?"

His brother nodded.

Max lowered his voice. "Noemi is pregnant. I'm going to be a father."

"You are?" Confusion flickered in his brother's eyes. "But how? The doctors said that isn't possible."

"I know. But it's true. She's pregnant." A smile pulled at Max's lips. "Miracles do happen."

"Why haven't you told anyone?"

"It's complicated. Noemi and I are still getting used to the idea."

"Are you sure it's yours?"

Max nodded. "Definitely. But as you can imagine, it wasn't planned." He pleaded with his eyes. "Please don't say anything to anyone. The situation is delicate. Noemi and I haven't decided how to handle this. I told you this so you wouldn't worry so much. This will all work out."

"I hope you're right."

So did he. There were still so many unknowns about his father's health, the state of the country and what Noemi planned to do next. But right now Max surprised himself by stepping up to the plate to help—could it be that preparing for fatherhood was preparing him for taking over the responsibility and care of his country?

CHAPTER FOURTEEN

IT JUST WASN'T the same.

Not without Max.

Though Gemma and her family were the nicest people, Noemi missed Max. She assured herself it was because they were becoming good friends. Nothing more.

Noemi returned to the palace to find another note in her room from Max. Excitement coursed through her body when she read his handwritten note telling her to meet him in the blue room at six thirty. She glanced at the clock on the mantel. That wasn't far from now.

Her gaze returned to the note. The blue room? She didn't remember visiting it on her tour of the palace. She wondered if this dinner would go better with his mother. She'd been a bit friendlier at their last meeting. Noemi hoped their relationship would continue to improve since they would play some sort of role in other's lives once the baby was born.

Noemi rushed to the wardrobe and flung

open the doors. She shouldn't have stayed in the village for so long, but for the first time since her parents had passed away, she had that sense of family—of belonging. The residents of Ostania were so friendly and welcoming.

Her gaze scanned over the selection of dresses she'd bought in the village. Red—too daring. Black—already wore the color. Green—too short. Silver—too casual. Why had they all looked so good when she'd picked them out?

A bit of blue lace called to her. She pulled out the dress. Long lace sleeves led to a modest neckline. But the blue chiffon skirt was short. Too short? But she was out of options.

She wore her hair loose and swept off to the side. She took extra care in applying her makeup, not putting on too much. She looked in the mirror and knew she wouldn't fit in this conservative household. If Max was hoping she'd change, he was in for a reality check. Max would have to accept her the way she was. Not that she needed his acceptance or that of his family's. She wasn't princess material.

With a second and then a third glance in the mirror, she assured herself that she hadn't forgotten anything. Then she let herself out the door. It was time to go find the blue room. She didn't want to be late.

In the hallway, she glanced around for someone to ask directions. She looked up and down the hallway, but there wasn't anyone around. How could that be? There were always people going here and there with their arms full of cleaning supplies or fresh linens, but when she needed them, none were about.

She recalled Max saying that all the public rooms were on the first floor and so that's where she would start. Although in a palace this size, it would take her all evening to search the rooms.

At the bottom of the steps, she peeked in the first room. There was no one in it. The next was vacant and the walls were red. And so she continued down the hallway, checking each room.

When she stepped into a room with cream walls, she found it wasn't vacant. An older woman, with her white hair up in a bun and wearing a black uniform, looked over from where she was drawing the curtains.

The woman turned to her and gave her appearance a quick once-over. "May I help you, ma'am?"

"I was looking for the blue room."

The woman's brows momentarily lifted.

"Ma'am, the blue room is in the west tower on the second floor."

The woman went on to explain how to get there and Noemi appreciated it because she never would have found it any other way. There were so many hallways and doorways that a person could easily get lost in here. Noemi resisted the urge to ask the woman for a map.

When Noemi reached what she hoped was the right tower, she poked her head inside the doorway. It was then that she noticed a candlelit table near the windows. She took a step into the room. "Max?"

"Over here." He was standing in front of the windows wearing a dark suit and tie. He looked like he'd just walked off the pages of some glamor magazine. And the way he looked at her made her knees turn jelly soft. It was all she could do to stand up.

"I… I had a little trouble finding you. I hope I'm not late." She glanced around, looking for the rest of his family.

"You're right on time. And sorry. I totally forgot to put directions in the note. I was distracted."

"Where is everyone else?"

"Everyone else?"

"Yes." When he sent her a puzzle look, she added, "You know, your family."

"They aren't coming. This is a dinner for two."

It was then that her gaze moved to the table set for two. There were candles and flowers. "What is all this?"

"Just an apology."

"Apology? For what?" She couldn't think of anything he'd done wrong. In fact, he'd been quite charming.

"For abandoning you today. I wouldn't have left if I didn't have to. I hope you know that."

She nodded. "Did everything work out for you?"

He didn't say anything at first. "It went as well as could be expected."

She approached him. "That doesn't sound so good." She stopped when she was in front of him and lifted her chin until their gazes met. She could see storm clouds of emotions reflected in his eyes. The meeting must have been much worse than he was anticipating.

"What is it?" she asked. "You can talk to me."

"You'd really be interested in hearing about state business?"

She nodded, wanting to be included.

And so Max started to fill her in on how the country's economy was being jeopardized by their insistence on following tradition. Ostania mainly exported agriculture goods such as vegetables, trees and seeds. They had some of the most exotic seeds in the world. But their insistence on relying on one form of export was making the global reach limited and in some cases it was shrinking.

Noemi looked at him thoughtfully for a moment. "So what you need is to broaden your country's expertise?"

He nodded. "But you seem to be the only one to really get this concept. The cabinet is insisting that this is merely an economic hiccup—a blip in the economy."

"But you think it's much more?"

"I do."

She took a sip of ice water as she considered his problem. "Have you considered retraining your people?"

"This country and its people are steeped in archaic traditions—whether they make sense or not. Most people won't consider changing the way things have always been done."

"Then start with the young people. These are the ones that strain against tradition."

"I've thought of that but once the progressives leave Ostania for higher education, they don't return."

"And that's where you're losing your country's most valuable resource. Have you considered opening your own university?"

A light of interest shone in his eyes. "And then we could gear the curriculum toward the future of Ostania."

"Something like that."

"You are brilliant. I will start plans for a university as soon as I am king. No." He shook his head. "It can't wait. This must be started immediately."

She loved being able to contribute to a solution that would help the country. And she loved it even more that Max took what she had to say seriously.

He smiled at her, but he didn't say anything.

Feeling a bit conspicuous, she asked, "Why are you smiling?"

"It's nice to have someone who gets what I'm saying."

She relaxed and smiled back at him. "And it's nice to have someone listen to me and take what I have to say seriously."

A look of concern came over his face. "Who doesn't take you seriously?"

"My family. Sometimes it's like I'm not even there. They talk right past me."

"I understand."

"You do?" He was probably just saying that to be nice. "But you're a prince, everyone must listen to you."

He shook his head. "After my infertility diagnosis, I became invisible as they rushed to groom my brother to assume the crown. It got so bad that I felt I... I just couldn't stand feeling so inadequate."

Her gaze met his. "You really do understand. I'm just so sorry for all you've gone through. And here I am complaining and what I've endured is nothing compared to you—"

"Don't do that. Your pain is no less important."

His words meant so much to her. "I became the face of Cattaneo Jewels by default. My family didn't know what else to do with me."

"I thought you were the face of the line because your beauty is absolutely stunning. Men can't help but stare at you. And women wish they were you. And by wearing Cattaneo Jewels, it's the closest they'll ever get to your amazing looks."

Noemi's mouth gaped. He surely hadn't meant all that. She forced her lips together. Had he? Because no other man had ever swept her off her feet with merely his words.

As though he could read her thoughts, he said, "Don't look at me like that. You have to know it's true. But there's so much more to you to admire, such as your generous heart and your smarts." He reached out, covering her hand with his. "I think we could make a great team."

She didn't know if he meant romantically or professionally, but either way, her heart beat faster as she gazed into his eyes. What would it be like to be his partner? The thought appealed to her on every level.

Just then a server entered the room carrying a tray of food. Noemi and Max pulled apart and her hand became noticeably cold where he'd once been touching her. The server placed the food on the table and quietly left.

Max pulled out a chair for Noemi. "I hope you don't mind that I chose dinner."

"I'm sure whatever you picked will be good."

They started with onion soup topped with sourdough bread and gruyere cheese. She had to admit that it was the best she'd ever had. The soup dishes were cleared and a plate of hardy greens with a lemon and garlic vinaigrette was placed before them.

Once Noemi finished her salad, she said, "I'm going to be too full for the main course."

"You're going to need all the energy you can get for what I have planned this evening."

Was he hitting on her? Suddenly her mind filled with images of them upstairs putting her king-size bed to good use. His lips pressed to hers. His hands touching her… She jerked her runaway thoughts to a halt. The heat of embarrassment rushed up her neck and set her cheeks ablaze.

"Noemi, are you okay?"

Not able to find her voice, she nodded.

And then a smile eased the worry lines on Max's face. "Did you think I was planning to have my way with you?"

"Are you?"

He laughed. That wasn't the reaction she was expecting. Was the thought of making love to her again that preposterous? A rush of emotions had her eyes growing misty. Before the baby, she wasn't the wishy-washy type. She blinked repeatedly, refusing to give in to her pregnancy hormones.

Suddenly a look of dawning came over Max's face. "Hey, I didn't mean anything by that thoughtless comment. You already know how much I enjoy making love to you. I thought I made that quite clear. But if you'd like me to remind you—"

"No." The response came too fast and too loudly. They both knew she was lying. She stared into his eyes, seeing that he was being perfectly honest. "I… I'm just feeling a little emotional right now."

"I've read that about pregnant women."

"You've been reading about my pregnancy?"

He nodded. "You had a good idea about learning as much as we can before that little guy—"

"Or little girl."

He smiled. "Or little girl gets here. Anyway, I will try to watch what I say in the future. Are we okay?"

She nodded. "But you never said what you had in mind for this evening."

"That's right. I didn't."

"Well…"

"It's a surprise."

The server returned with the main course, *pot-au-feu*. Noemi inhaled the inviting aroma of the beef and vegetable stew. It was perfect for a cold winter evening. She gave it her best effort but she couldn't finish all of it.

She pushed the plate back. "I'm sorry. I am so full."

"Does that mean you don't want some bubbly and dessert?"

"First, I can't have bubbly—"

"You can if it's sparkling grape juice."

She smiled at his thoughtfulness. "Do you think of everything?"

"No. But I try. I want you to enjoy your visit to Ostania."

"It's really important to you, isn't it?"

He nodded. "So dessert can wait." He got to his feet and held his hand out to her. "Shall we go?"

She placed her hand in his and stood. "Go where?"

His eyes twinkled. "You'll see."

She followed his lead as they made their way toward the rear of the palace. By the back door, he stopped. On a chair near the door sat a white box. Max picked it up and held it out to her.

"What's this?" She loved presents. Her parents always made sure there were plenty of presents under the Christmas tree. "An early Christmas present?"

"If you want it to be."

While he continued to hold the box, she removed the gold tie and lifted the lid. Inside were a pair of white ice skates. Her gaze moved from the present to Max. "You got me skates?"

He nodded. "Do you like them?"

"Yes. But I didn't get you anything." She had no idea he was planning to give her anything. "It's not Christmas yet."

"I wanted to get a jump start on the holiday."

And then she noticed her coat resting on the back of the chair. "What are you up to?"

"Put on your coat and you'll find out." He paused and his forehead creased as his gaze skimmed over her short dress. "On second thought, would you like to change? It's cold outside."

She glanced down at her exposed legs. "I'll be right back."

Noemi took off for her room, all the while trying to remember her way back to this spot. When she reached her room, her cell phone rang. She considered ignoring it as she was anxious to get back to Max. But then she checked the caller ID. It was Leo.

"Hey, Leo. Is something wrong?"

"No. I'm just checking in. Are you still in Mont Coeur?"

"After you left, I decided to take a little trip, but I will be back for Christmas. You're still planning to be there, right?" When the only response was silence, she said, "Please, Leo. This is really important to me. I want to get to know you. We're family and we should spend our first Christmas together."

"Okay. If it means that much to you—"

"It does."

They chatted a few more minutes while she located her leggings and then shimmied into them. With a promise to see each other next week, they ended the call.

Noemi dashed out the door and down the hallway, hoping she didn't get lost. And then she came upon Max texting on his phone while he waited for her. He lifted his head and smiled. Her stomach felt as though a swarm of butterflies had taken flight within it.

They both put on their coats and headed outside. It was then that she noticed the ice skating rink had been lit up with thousands of white twinkle lights. She hadn't recalled noticing the lights before. Was this another detail Max had seen to? The lights reflected off the ice and made the snow on the sides look like a million sparkling diamonds.

She turned to him. "You did all this?"

"The ice skating rink was already set up. It's part of our tradition."

"But the lights. I don't remember seeing them the other day. It looks…" She paused taking it all in. "It looks magical."

It looks romantic. Just like the dinner.

"I have to admit that I did have the lights put up. I noticed in Mont Coeur that you like Christmas lights."

"I do. I love them."

They moved to the edge of the skate rink and laced up their skates. Max knelt in front of her and made sure her skates were tied properly. When he stood, he held his hand out to her. She placed her hand in his and let him help her to her feet.

"Come on. I'll show you how to skate." Max stepped onto the ice.

How did he get the idea that she couldn't skate? She thought of saying something but resisted. She decided to let him take the lead. She enjoyed the touch of his hands and the nearness of his body.

"Don't worry," he said. "I've got you. I won't let you fall."

Maybe she should fess up about her ability to skate. "You don't have to do this—"

"But I want to. There's so much I want to share with you."

She was pretty certain they were no longer talking about skating. As she continued to stare deep into his eyes, she said, "I'd like that."

"Do you feel steady on the skates?"

She nodded. "You really want to show me, don't you?"

"Yes. We'll take it slow. Take a step. Another step. And then glide."

She did exactly as he said. She could so clearly imagine him being a good parent and patient teacher with their child. They continued around the rink slowly. After the second pass, Max picked up the pace a little.

"You're doing great." He smiled at her. "Instead of being a prince, perhaps I should become a skate instructor."

"You're looking for a career change?" She knew he wasn't serious, but part of her wondered if he was just an ordinary citizen whether their lives would mesh.

"Maybe." His voice cut through her meandering thoughts. "What do you think? Want to give me an endorsement?"

"I don't know how much help I would be. Anybody would be excited to skate with a prince."

"I'm not so sure about that."

She gazed up at him, noticing the smile had fled his face. "I am. You're an amazing man. You're thoughtful, sweet and strong. This country is lucky to have you."

His gaze probed hers. "And how about you? Do you feel lucky to have me in your life?

Back when they'd collided on the sidewalk in Mont Coeur with the crush of fans, her answer might have been different. But since then she'd learned the tabloid headlines were not accurate. Max was nothing like the sensational gossip.

"Yes, I'm lucky. And so is our baby." She meant every word.

On the fourth loop, Max said, "Would you like to try it on your own?"

"Do you think I should?"

"Go ahead. I'll be right here." And then he let go of her hands.

The cold seeped in where he'd once been holding her. She took a step, getting her bearings without his steady grasp. It had been a few years since she'd been skating, but as she took one step after the next, it all came back to her like riding a bike.

She moved past Max. The cool air swished over her face and combed through her hair. She picked up pace and soon she was gliding over the ice.

When she looped back around, she found Max standing there staring at her. She did a spin and came to a stop in front of him. A look of surprise came over Max's face. She couldn't tell if that was a good or bad sign.

"You know how to skate?"

She nodded. "I've been skating since I was a little girl."

"But I didn't think you did."

"You didn't ask. And you were so sweet about it. I... I didn't want to ruin the moment. I hope you're not mad."

He shook his head as he moved closer to her. "What else don't I know about you?"

"My parents loved the holidays. They loved skiing, but they would indulge my passion for ice skating." Talking about her parents filled her with deep sorrow and regret.

Max skated in front of her and took her hands in his. "What's wrong?"

Noemi pulled away from him. She clasped her hands together. The mention of her parents brought back a barrage of memories—some of them good but then there was their final conversation.

"Noemi, what's wrong?" The concern rang out in Max's voice. "If I said or did anything wrong—"

"No. It's not you. It's me." She skated to the edge of the ice.

He followed her. "I don't understand." He

took her hand and led her to a nearby bench. "I hope you know that you can talk to me about anything."

She gazed up at the twinkle lights. "When I found out I was pregnant and I didn't know how to contact you, I visited the Cattaneo Jewels headquarters in Milan. Not having anyone to turn to, I told my parents I was pregnant. They didn't take it well. They made me feel like…like I'd let them down. It was terrible."

"I'm sorry. I should have been there. I never should have walked away from you that morning without knowing your full name and your phone number. If I could go back in time and change things, please believe me I would."

"I would change that, too."

Max's head dipped and his lips caught hers. It was a quick kiss but it said so much. His touch was a balm upon her heart.

Noemi pulled back. She needed to get this all out. "While I was at my parents' offices, I was handed a piece of mail. I didn't know it at the time but it wasn't meant for me—it was intended for my mother. We share the same initials. Anyway, I opened it and found a letter from my brother Leo. At the time, though, I didn't know I had another brother. He was writing to my mother to agree to meet his biological parents."

Max reached out and placed his hand on hers. "That must have been quite a shock."

She took comfort in his touch. "It was devastating. I hate to admit it, but I didn't take it very well. I just didn't understand how my parents could keep such an important secret from Sebastian and me."

"Noemi, you don't have to tell me this if it's too painful."

She shook her head as she attempted to get her emotions under control. She swallowed past the lump in her throat. "Sebastian and I never had a really close relationship. With him being older and not sharing the same interests, he never had time for me. And then to learn that I had another brother—a brother that my parents kept a secret—it hurt. A lot."

"I can't even imagine what that must have been like."

"When I took the letter to my parents and confronted them about Leo, we argued. I couldn't understand how they could have been so hard on me when they'd also had an unplanned pregnancy. I…" Her voice faltered.

"Noemi?"

"I told them I never wanted to speak to them

again." She swiped at a tear as it slipped down her cheek. "And…and a few days later, they died in a helicopter crash on their way to meet Leo." One tear followed another. Her voice cracked with emotion. "Now I can never take back those words. I can never tell them that I'm sorry. That I love them."

"Shh…" He pulled her to him and held her until her emotions were under control. "Your parents knew you didn't mean it. They loved you. They wanted to find their other son because the bond with a child is stronger than anything, and they died united in their love for one another and for their family. And that's what I want—I want to unite our family."

And then without another word, Max lowered his head and caught her lips with his. Her heart fluttered in her chest. There, beneath the starry sky and twinkling lights, a prince was kissing her. This had to be a fairy tale.

His arm slipped over her shoulders, pulling her to his side. She willingly followed his lead. As his mouth moved over hers, deepening the kiss, she let go of the reasons this wouldn't work between them. For this moment—this night, nothing seemed impossible.

When he pulled back, he ran his fingers over her cheek. "You're cold. We should go inside."

She hadn't noticed the cold. Snuggled to him, she was quite warm. But she was in absolutely no mood to argue. "If you think that would be best."

"I do."

He made quick work of switching back into his shoes. He told her to wait and he'd be right back. He disappeared into the palace. She had no idea what he was up to. It was a night of surprises.

Noemi finished switching shoes and was just about to step inside the palace when Max swung the door open. He had nothing in his hands, but he wore an expression that said he had something planned.

"What did you do?" She stepped inside.

Max shrugged his shoulders and feigned a totally innocent expression as they headed toward her suite of rooms. "Nothing."

Just the way he said it told her that he was most definitely up to something.

"Max?" She couldn't help but smile. Being with him made her happy and she didn't want it to end. "Just tell me."

"Why do you think I did something?"

"Because this night, it has been amazing. And…" She stopped on the landing and turned to him. "I don't want the evening to end."

This time she lifted up on her tiptoes and pressed her lips to his. The kiss was brief, but there was a promise of more—oh, so much more.

When she pulled back, she took his hand and continued up the steps. His thumb rubbed over the back of her hand, sending the most delicious sensations throughout her body. Was it just a prelude to something more?

'Thank you for tonight," she said, as they headed down the long, quiet hallway. "It was the most amazing evening."

When he spoke, his voice took on a deep timbre. "And it's not over yet."

A shiver of excitement raced over her skin. "What do you have in mind?"

"We haven't had dessert yet."

That wasn't what she'd been thinking of, but she was curious as to what he had planned. "What is dessert?"

"You'll see." He swung her bedroom door open.

Max gestured for her to go first. The lights were dimmed. Inside was a table with two tapered candles, whose flames flickered. She moved to the table. There was a bowl full of plump strawberries and a bowl of whipped cream. Off to the side was an ice bucket with a bottle of sparkling grape juice and two flutes.

When she turned to Max, he closed the door and approached her. "I hope you like berries."

"I love them." She loved everything. Most of all, she loved that he'd gone to so much trouble for her. "But how did you get them in the winter?"

He smiled. "Being a prince does have its advantages."

"It does, huh?" She turned, picked up a strawberry and dunked it in the whipped cream. She turned back to him and held out the berry.

He bit the berry. Then he did the same for her, only she moved at the wrong moment and some whipped cream ended up on the side of her mouth. When she moved to clean it, Max brushed her hand aside. He leaned forward and licked the whipped cream from the side of her mouth. Then his tongue traced around her lips.

A moan escaped her lips. The dessert was so very sweet. And she wasn't thinking about the berries and cream. This was going to be the best night of her life.

CHAPTER FIFTEEN

THE NEXT MORNING, Noemi woke up with a smile.

Her hand moved to the other side of the bed. The spot was empty and the pillow was cold. But Max's imprint was there. And when she rolled over, she could still smell Max's intoxicating scent on the linens.

When her gaze strayed across the time on the clock, she groaned. It was after nine. She'd slept in. No wonder Max wasn't around. She was being a total slacker and yet there was nowhere she had to be until lunch. That's the time she'd agreed to meet Gemma's mother. They were going to grab lunch in the village and then visit the local botanical gardens. She was told it was decorated for Christmas and quite a sight to behold.

She slipped out of bed and rushed through the shower. She was certain that she'd missed breakfast, but she hoped she could grab something to tide her over until lunch. Her stomach growled in agreement. This pregnancy stuff had certainly increased her appetite.

Wearing another pair of leggings and a long flowing top, she rushed back into the bedroom to find Max at the table with a covered dish sitting opposite him. He paused from flipping through a manila folder full of papers to give her his full attention.

"Good morning, beautiful. I wanted to make sure you got something to eat." He set the folder aside.

Heat rushed to her cheeks. "Why didn't you wake me up?"

"You were sleeping so soundly. I didn't want to disturb you."

"I would have gladly woken up." She leaned forward and pressed a quick kiss to his lips. When she pulled back, she noticed the worried look on his face. "What's wrong?"

Max forced a smile on his face but it didn't ease the worry lines. "I can't spend the day with you. I'm sorry."

"It's okay. But you'll still be able to make it to the doctor's appointment this evening, won't you?"

"Nothing could keep me away."

Noemi breathed a little easier. She was worried about the baby for no particular reason other than she'd just read a chapter about all the potential complications of pregnancy. Once she saw the baby and heard its heartbeat, she'd feel much better.

"Then stop feeling bad," she said. "You'll be there for the important part."

"Being with you is important, too. I asked you here so that we could spend more time together. And now I have to bail on you. Again."

"Stop. I'm not upset. See." Noemi pointed to the smile on her face. "I'm good. I'm great. In fact, I have plans for today."

"You do?"

She nodded. "I'm planning to meet up with Gemma and her mother. We're going to visit the botanical garden. There's a Christmas display."

He stood and took her in his arms. "I was planning to take you there. I think you'll be very impressed with the display."

"I understand about you not being able to go, but I will miss you."

"It won't be long until we're together again for your doctor's appointment. Just a few hours. I promise."

He leaned down and pressed his lips to hers. Her heart pounded just like it had when they'd kissed for the first time. Something told her that no matter how many times he kissed her, it would always be special—like the first time.

The day would have been a lot more fun having him along. It was the first time that she acknowledged just how much she enjoyed Max's company. If his goal had been for them to grow closer, it was definitely working.

But what would happen when this fantasy vacation ended?

Max couldn't get the images of Noemi out of his mind.

Kissing her.

Holding her.

Their night together had been better than the first time. It had bridged the distance between them. It had Max even more determined to make her his princess.

And then there was Noemi's growing baby bump. Now, as they stood in the examination room of the doctor's office, Max was filled with this sense of awe over the baby followed by a wave of unconditional love. In that moment, it really drove home the fact that in just a few months he would become a father.

And what would happen when it came time for Noemi to return to Mont Coeur? Each day they were growing closer, but would it be enough to convince her to stay? How else could he convince her that they could make this work? That he would do whatever it took to make her happy—

"Max?" Noemi's voice jarred him out of his thoughts. When he sent her a puzzled look, she said, "The doctor wants to know if you have any questions before we begin the scan."

Max shook his head.

As Noemi leaned back on the exam table, she gave him another strange look. It was as though she wanted to probe further, but she thought better of it in front of the doctor. Dr. Roussel had been around a long time—long enough to deliver his brother and himself.

However, the man was one to stay on top of technology, which was why Max trusted him with caring for Noemi and their baby. The doctor was also known for his discretion.

After the doctor squeezed some gel on Noemi's expanding abdomen, he ran a wand over her skin. Max watched everything intently, making sure nothing went wrong. Somewhere along the way, Noemi's hand ended up in his as they watched the monitor.

"There is your baby." Dr. Roussel pointed to the screen.

The breath caught in the back of Max's throat.

That little white smudge on the screen was his son or daughter. He would never again say he didn't believe in miracles.

Max smiled brightly and then looked at Noemi. "Are you crying?"

She looked at him. "You are, too."

With his free hand, he felt the dampness on his cheeks. And so he was. But they were tears of joy.

"This is the head." The doctor pointed it out. "And this is the spine. And…"

The doctor's voice faded away as he continued to study the monitor. Then he grew quiet as he moved the wand. For the longest time, the doctor didn't say anything. He studied the image this way and that way. And then he started to take measurements.

Max looked at Noemi, whose joy had ebbed away and was replaced by a frightened look. So he wasn't the only one?

"Is something wrong?" Noemi asked.

Max couldn't find his voice because he was too busy praying that his son or daughter was all right. He was even willing to make a deal with God for the baby to be healthy.

"Everything is all right." The doctor turned to Noemi and smiled. "Your baby is healthy. I'm just checking something that might explain your rapidly expanding waistline and increased appetite."

Max's gaze caught Noemi's. She looked hesitant to relax. The doctor was being cryptic and that was not reassuring.

"Doctor—"

Dr. Roussel waved him off. "I just about have it." He moved the wand a little bit. "Yes, it's just as I suspected."

"What is it?" Max asked, staring at the monitor, not sure what he was seeing.

"It's this right here." Dr. Roussel pointed to an image. "And this right here." He pointed to another image.

"What is it?" Noemi's voice was a bit high-pitched.

Dr. Roussel turned with a reassuring smile. "Those, my dear, are your twins."

"Twins?" Max felt a bit light-headed. His legs felt rubbery. He was glad there was a stool beside him. He sank down on it.

"Yes," the doctor answered. "See here." He pointed to the monitor. "That is baby number one's heart beating. And that is baby number two's. I'll turn on the speaker."

They heard one heartbeat. It was a strong whoosh-whoosh sound. The other heartbeat was softer. The doctor assured them that was natural.

When Max looked at Noemi, her face was wet with tears. He leaned over to her and kissed her gently on the lips. "You are amazing."

"Twins." Noemi's voice was filled with awe. "Do you know if we're having boys or girls? Or one of each?"

As the doctor wiped the gel from her abdomen, he said, "I'm afraid it's too early for anything definitive, but they should be able to tell you at your next appointment."

Max felt as though this was part of some sort of dream. Twins. That seemed so unreal. Sure, there were twins on his mother's side of the family, but he never thought it was a possibility because he wasn't supposed to have children in the first place.

When they were ready to go, Dr. Roussel handed them some paperwork and photos. "Here are pictures from the scan. They are both the same. One for each of you." And then the doctor said to Max, "Your parents are going to be so happy. This is the kind of news they could use right now."

Noemi sent him a puzzled look as Max had yet to find a good time to tell her about his father's condition or the fact that the king had been put on the organ donor list. And there was a more selfish reason. Telling her would make it real. Everything in his life was changing at once and he was having problems keeping his footing.

He would tell her everything, very soon.

The following morning, Max found himself stuck in another cabinet meeting. All his plans for Noemi's visit were ruined. And yet he couldn't turn his back on his responsibilities. Maybe it was the worry over his father's condition or learning he was about to be a father of twins, but he wanted to pitch in.

"Your Highness?" A royal advisor peered at Max over the top of his spectacles.

Max had lost track of the conversation about the sudden dip in Ostania's economy—a problem that could have a devastating effect for everyone in the nation if it wasn't dealt with swiftly. The whole cabinet was in the meeting, including his brother, Tobias. The only empty chair was his father's.

"Why are you looking to me for the answers?" Max asked, feeling as though he was missing something. "You should be talking to my brother."

"With your father under the influence of

medication, his heir needs to make the decision."

Max glanced around the room. "And we all know that is Tobias."

"Do we?" the elder advisor asked.

He knew. Max's gaze moved around the room from one person to the next. The whole cabinet knew Noemi was pregnant. Max's body tensed. This wasn't good—not at all. Noemi wasn't prepared for what was to come.

And there was only one way the cabinet could know about Noemi's pregnancy. Max turned an accusatory stare at his brother.

Tobias cleared his throat. "I need to speak with my brother in private. Can you give us the room?"

The elder advisor looked as though he was going to protest when Tobias gave him a very stern look, silencing the man's words.

Once all the people had moved to the hallway and closed the door, Tobias turned to Max. "You need to tell them."

"Tell them what?"

"About the baby. That you are the legitimate heir to the throne."

Max shook his head. "No."

"Max—"

"I said no. It isn't the right time."

"I don't understand. I would think you'd be shouting this from the palace towers for all the world to hear. You aren't having doubts about the baby, are you?"

"The baby happens to be twins—"

"Twins?" Tobias smiled brightly. "That's awesome. Twice the babies to spoil."

Tobias gave him a hug and clapped him on the back. Max longed to tell everyone the great news but he had to be patient and so did his brother.

"Wait until you tell Mother—"

"Slow down. Noemi isn't ready for all that. She's still getting used to the idea of us and now she has to adjust to the idea of twins."

"Well, I have something to admit." Tobias at least had the decency to look guilty. "The cabinet knows."

"I thought as much." Max frowned at his brother.

This couldn't be happening. He'd been waiting for the right time to make the announcement. This wasn't it. But if the news was out, he could help run the country. He could lift the burden from his father and brother. He would talk to Noemi later. He'd fix this...somehow.

CHAPTER SIXTEEN

SHE NEEDED TO find Max. She couldn't wait.

After checking with everyone she passed in the palace, Noemi finally got his whereabouts from the butler. She had big news; the babies had moved. It was the first time she'd been able to feel them. It was the most amazing experience. And she needed to share it with Max.

She rushed down the hallway, glancing in each room that she passed. Max was going to be so excited. The babies were getting bigger.

And she was growing closer to Max all the time. She could talk to him and he listened. Just like in the village when Gemma had been lost, he'd listened to her.

Max was everything she could want in a man. He was thoughtful and caring. Maybe they could be more than co-parents. Her heart fluttered at the thought of him taking a more prominent, more romantic role in her life.

As such, she wanted to invite him back to Mont Coeur for Christmas. She wanted him to meet her brothers. She knew it might not be the smoothest of holidays and she would feel so much better if Max was there next to her.

As she turned the corner, she found a group of men standing in the spacious hallway. The voices echoed in the hallway. And then someone said Max's name.

Noemi paused next to a large potted palm plant. Something just seemed off to her. Max was nowhere to be seen and yet they were talking about him. It was probably nothing, but still she stayed in place.

"Prince Maximilian told Prince Tobias that we'd have to wait a couple more weeks before they can do an in-utero test to confirm the parentage of the baby. Once it's legally confirmed, we can proceed with plans for Prince Maximilian to take over the throne. At last, it will be the way it was supposed to be all along."

"And the prince? Is he certain this is his baby?"

"He said he needs the test to be sure. The sooner, the better."

Noemi's heart sank the whole way down to her black heels. Her word hadn't been good enough for Max. She moved until her back was against the wall. She needed the support to keep her on her feet.

All this time he'd had doubts.

Once again, her words didn't carry any validity.

Her heart felt as though it was being torn in two. She'd never felt so devastated—so angry. Tears pricked the back of her eyes, but she blinked them away. Giving into her emotions would have to wait. She had things to do now. She wouldn't stay where her word meant nothing.

The sound of a door opening had her glancing up.

"Gentlemen, let's continue the meeting. My brother and I would like to discuss the best way to make this transfer of control once we have the test results."

It was Max's voice. And he'd just confirmed what the men had said. The breath caught in her throat. She didn't move. She just couldn't face him now. She was afraid she would say something that she couldn't take back. And no matter what she was feeling in this moment, she had to think of the babies.

The men were moving away from her. When at last the door snicked shut, Noemi blew out an uneven breath. It was as if she were waking up from a dream and reality was so harsh.

Her feet started to move, retracing her steps.

She had to get away. She had to make sense of all this. The kisses. The steamy looks. The dinners. Were they all just some ploy? Did he feel nothing for her?

Her head started to pound. Her steps came faster and faster. She forced herself to slow down. She didn't want anyone to think that something was wrong. She didn't want to explain that she'd made an utter fool of herself—falling for a prince with nothing but power on his mind.

Everything would work out.

Max rotated his shoulders, trying to ease the kink in his neck. The meeting with the cabinet had been long and at times contentious. But in the end, it was best that the news of the twins was out. He was able to lift a lot of stress off his younger brother and he was able to fill in for his father who had just started dialysis.

Now it was time he talked to Noemi. Everything they'd arranged in the meeting hinged on her agreeing to do a paternity test. Otherwise, the bulk of responsibility would be thrown back at his brother and that just wasn't fair—not when Max was in the position to do the right thing.

But first, he needed a hug and a long tantalizing kiss. Just the thought of holding Noemi in his arms again had him moving faster up the steps until he was taking them two at a time.

When he reached her bedroom door, he rapped his knuckles on it. Then he opened the door and stepped inside, expecting to find Noemi. She was nowhere to be seen.

He checked the time. It was going on seven in the evening. Would she be in the village this late? Maybe Gemma's family invited her to dinner. It wasn't like he expected her to sit around, waiting for him.

He was about to turn and leave when his gaze strayed across an envelope propped up on the nightstand table. Was that his name on it? He took a step closer. It was.

A smile lifted his lips. He imagined there was a love note inside. The idea appealed to him. He'd never had anyone write him a love letter before. Warmth filled his chest—a feeling he'd never known before Noemi. She'd brought so many amazing firsts to his life.

With his hopes up, he stuck his finger in the top of the envelope and ripped. He slipped out the piece of paper. He couldn't wait to see what it had to say.

Max,

I've gone back to Mont Coeur. I know that you've told everyone about the twins and I'm not willing to go along with this. You only have your own interests at heart— not what's best for me or our babies. I refuse to be a "silent partner" in both my own and our twins' lives. Please don't follow me. I need time to think. I'll send you updates on the babies.

Some of the words were smudged as though tears had smeared the ink.

How had this happened? How did she know when he'd just found out about his brother spreading the news? Had Tobias said something in front of the help? Even so, they were usually so discreet.

He gave himself a mental shake. It didn't matter how she found out. It only mattered how he got her back. If he could speak to her, she would understand. Wouldn't she?

CHAPTER SEVENTEEN

HOME SWEET HOME.

Although Noemi didn't feel the comfort that the luxury chalet normally gave her. In fact, she'd barely slept the night before. That morning, the sun shone brightly, reflecting off the snow, but it didn't cheer her up.

Noemi didn't bother turning on the Christmas lights. She wasn't in the mood to be jolly. She hadn't had morning sickness in quite a while, but right now her stomach was sour and her head pounded.

She couldn't believe she'd been so wrong about Max. She'd thought he was such a nice guy. She'd thought that the news sources had gotten him wrong. He wasn't out for himself—he cared about others. Boy, had she been wrong.

Knock. Knock.

She wasn't expecting anyone. When she'd arrived last night, neither of her brothers were here. Christmas wasn't until next week. Maybe

Leo had arrived early. After all, this was now his home, too. And maybe it would be better not to rattle around this big place by herself.

She swung open the door and the words of greeting stuck to her tongue.

Max stood there with red roses in hand. Flowers weren't going to fix this problem.

"You shouldn't be here." Noemi attempted to close the door.

Max stuck his foot in the way. "I flew all this way. Won't you even hear me out?"

She let go of the door and walked into the living room. Maybe it was best to have it all out now. Behind her, she heard the door close followed by approaching footsteps. She moved to the other side of the room and turned. She leveled her shoulders and crossed her arms. And then she waited.

"I…uh…brought these for you." He held out the roses. When she didn't move to take them, he placed them on the wooden coffee table.

When he straightened, his gaze caught hers. She refused to turn away. She hadn't done anything wrong here.

"Aren't you going to say anything?" he asked.

"You're the one that flew here after I told you I needed time. It's up to you to talk."

Max slipped off his coat and then rubbed the

back of his neck. "You shouldn't have just left. If you'd waited and talked to me, we could have worked it out."

She shook her head. "No, we couldn't."

"You're overreacting."

"No. I'm not. I know what I heard."

He held up his hands in surrender as he sank down on the couch. "I didn't come here to fight with you."

"Then why did you come?"

"To tell you that I want you—" He stopped himself, shook his head and then started again. "I came here to *ask* you to be by my side as I ascend to the throne."

Not I love you. Or I'm sorry.

Noemi shook her head. "I don't want our children to be used as some bargaining chip to give you an easy path to the crown."

Max sat straight up. "That's not what I'm doing. There's been a lot going on at the palace—things I haven't told you. It's important that the babies are tested as soon as it's safe and then I can assume my position as the heir to the throne."

"You aren't listening. This isn't all about you. There's also the babies and myself to consider. Or don't we count?"

"Of course you do. And if you would just

hear me out, you would understand how important the test is."

He was so focused on the throne and that blasted test that he wasn't hearing her. He was acting the same way as her family—making her a silent partner in her own life. How had she missed seeing this before?

Her heart ached over the future they wouldn't have. She drew in a deep steadying breath. "Do you know what hurts the most?" She didn't wait for him to say anything. "It's that after the loss of my parents—the loss of my mother— I thought that I'd finally found someone that I could count on. Someone I could lean on. Someone who'd listen to me."

"You did. I'm here for you." His eyes pleaded with her.

She shook her head. "Not when your sole focus is becoming king. Now, please go."

Max got to his feet. He looked at her. His mouth opened but no words came out. And then he turned and walked out the door.

Noemi didn't know whether to be relieved that he'd left without a fight or hurt that he'd given up on them so easily.

CHAPTER EIGHTEEN

HE WASN'T GIVING UP. He was regrouping.

Max strode back and forth in the condo he'd rented for the night. On this trip, he'd broken with protocol and traveled alone. He needed privacy in order to fix what he'd broken.

He walked away the night before because they both needed to catch their breath. He hadn't expected such resistance to the idea of her coming back to Ostania and having the babies tested. He thought she liked it in Ostania. She had been making friends.

He continued to pace.

He was not giving up.

And that was something new for him. After his cancer diagnosis, he gave up. And yet he went into remission and since then he'd been deemed cured. And when he was told he couldn't have children—he couldn't live up to his birthright—he'd given up and left Ostania, left the palace life. This time when things weren't going his way, he refused to give up— to walk away.

He realized how much he wanted to stand up and take responsibility. He wanted to help his country. And at the same time, he wanted his family. He wanted Noemi.

He was being torn in two different directions. In that moment, he acknowledged that he couldn't live without Noemi and the twins. If he had to, he'd give up his claim to the throne.

He grabbed his coat and raced out the door. He had to tell Noemi that he chose her. He would always choose her.

The fresh snow from the night before slowed him down as he maneuvered his rented vehicle. Max stepped on the gas pedal harder than he should have and the back end fishtailed. He lifted his foot off the gas until the car straightened out. His back teeth ground together as he smothered a groan. He just wanted to get to Noemi as fast as possible. The longer this thing festered, the worse it would get.

Each second that passed felt like an hour. He wanted to tell Noemi that he chose her—that he loved her. It was the first time he'd been brave enough to admit it to himself. It was true. He loved Noemi and those babies with all his heart.

At last, he pulled to a stop in front of her cha-let. He jumped out of the car and then realized he'd been in such a rush he'd forgotten to turn off the engine. Once he silenced the engine, he jogged to the front door.

Max pushed the doorbell once. Twice. Three times. "Noemi! Noemi!"

He paused and waited. Nothing.

She had to be here, didn't she? Surely she wouldn't have left. Would she?

His hand clenched and he pounded on the door. "Noemi, please. We need to talk."

Still nothing, but he sensed she was listening to him.

"Noemi, please open the door." He placed his palm against the door and lowered his head. "Noemi, I love you."

He heard the snick of the deadbolt. He lowered his hand and took a step back, not wanting to crowd her. And then the door swung open.

Noemi stood there. There were shadows under her eyes. And her face was devoid of makeup. Her hair was pulled back in a hap-hazard ponytail. And she was wearing a baggy T-shirt with some pink leggings. He wasn't the only one who'd had a bad night.

She stood there. Silent.

"Noemi, may I come in?"

"Do you really think that will change anything?" Her eyes said that she didn't think it would.

It was okay. He had enough faith for both of them. "Yes."

To his surprise, she stepped back and swung the door wide open. He brushed off the snow from his coat and hair and stepped inside. He deposited his coat on a chair in the foyer and then followed her to the living room. Noemi sat down and he did the same, leaving a respectable space between them.

He couldn't help but notice that once again all the Christmas lights were dark. He knew how much she loved the holiday. This told him that she wasn't all right with the current circumstances either.

Max turned to Noemi. She was staring down at her hands as she fidgeted with the hem of her shirt. This wasn't going to work. He needed her full attention.

He knelt down in front of her. "Noemi, I've made a mess of all this. And I'm sorry."

Her gaze lifted. "You are?"

He nodded. "And I want you to know that I didn't tell the royal cabinet about your pregnancy. But I did tell my brother. I know I shouldn't have. It's just that he was so upset and scared when he heard how sick our father is. I didn't think, I just reacted. Later, he went behind my back and told the cabinet."

"Wait. What's wrong with your father?"

Max drew in a deep breath and told her about his father's diabetes and the kidney damage as well as his father waiting for a new kidney on the organ donor list.

"So you told your brother because you were comforting him?" When Max nodded, she asked, "You didn't tell him because you wanted to reclaim your position as next in line for the throne?"

Max shook his head. "I wouldn't have done that."

"But it doesn't change the fact that the babies are the key to you having everything."

"I've done a lot of thinking—a lot of soul searching. And I've come to a decision." He drew in a deep steadying breath. "I love you."

"You do?"

He nodded. "And I don't want to live without you. If I need to choose, I choose you. You and our babies."

"You'd walk away from your birthright—from the crown?"

"I would if that's the only way I could have you in my life."

CHAPTER NINETEEN

HER HEART HAMMERED.

He was saying all the right things.

Noemi struggled to find her voice. She couldn't hear her thoughts for the beating of her heart. He'd picked her. He wanted her. He loved her.

She swallowed hard. "I love you, too."

Noemi leaned forward and pressed her lips to his. Max moved to sit on the couch and pulled her onto his lap. They kissed some more. She wondered if he could feel the beating of her heart. It felt as though it was going to burst with love.

When she pulled back, she slipped onto the couch cushion next to him. She rested her head on his shoulder. She knew they couldn't leave things like this. She couldn't expect him to walk away from his heritage for her. In the end, they'd both be unhappy.

"Noemi, do you think your parents would

have been pleased that you and I—that we are together?"

"You mean because you're a prince?"

"No. Because I love you so much. I didn't know it was possible to care this much for another person."

Noemi's chest filled with the warmth of love. "I think my parents would have approved of you. I wouldn't have given them a choice. I can't live without you either. I love you very much." Before he could say anything, she momentarily pressed a fingertip to his lips, causing his brows to rise. "And I could never ask you to give up your claim to the throne. You are a wonderful leader, caring, compassionate and determined. You will make an excellent king. But you have to know that I'm done being a silent partner. If we do this…" she gestured to him and her "…then I need your assurance that you won't take me for granted." When his lips parted, she held up a finger to once again silence him. "And I need to know that you'll hear me when I speak and you'll take my opinion into consideration."

She looked at him expectantly. He arched a questioning brow and she smiled. "Yes, you can speak now."

"See. I do know how to listen. And I promise we will be in this life's adventure together—as equals. What you say matters to me, whether it's to do with our relationship, our children or the running of the country."

Her heart swelled with love for this most amazing man. "How did I get so lucky?"

His thumb caressed her cheek. "I'm the one that's lucky."

Max moved away. She thought he was getting ready to kiss her, but instead, he got up from the couch. What was he doing? He moved to the foyer. Where was he going?

"Max?"

"Stay there. I'll be right back."

Seconds later, he rushed back into the room. He was smiling—a great big smile that lit up his eyes. He stopped in front of the Christmas tree and turned on the twinkle lights. "Come here."

Her pulse picked up its pace. "Max, what are you up to?"

"Just come here." He held one hand behind his back as he waved her over with his other hand.

Her heart pounded with a blend of excitement and anticipation. "If you have an early Christmas present, you have to wait. I don't have any presents wrapped for you."

"Just come here. Please." His eyes pleaded with her.

Without another word, she moved from the couch and joined him next to the tree. It was then that he dropped down on bended knee. Her eyes filled with tears of joy. Was this really happening?

He took her hand in his. "Noemi, I love you. I've loved you since that first night when I spotted you across the room. I never believed in love at first sight, but you've turned me into a believer. And I can't imagine my life without you in it."

She pressed a shaky hand to her gaping mouth.

He moved his hand from behind his back. And there, nestled in a black velvet box, was a stunning sapphire engagement ring. Noemi knew from her tour of the palace that the ring was in Ostania's royal colors.

"Noemi, will you please be my partner—because we'll decide everything together—be my lover—because I could never ever get enough of you—and be my wife—because I want to spend every single day of my life with you?"

After a lifetime of being relegated to a silent

partner and not having her thoughts or feelings heard, Max had presented her with a proposal she couldn't turn down. Hand in hand, heart to heart, they would step into the future as equals.

She didn't hesitate. "Yes." Tears of joy raced down her face. "Yes. Yes."

Max stood up and pressed his lips to hers.

CHAPTER TWENTY

THE STAGE WAS SET.

The Christmas tree twinkled and carols played softly in the background.

Noemi glanced around the great room at Mont Coeur. Evening had settled on the resort and Max had started a fire. It crackled and popped in the large fireplace, casting the room in a warm glow.

She couldn't help but miss her parents. Her father had always taken charge of the fireplace and her mother had made sure there was something delicious to eat. Family gatherings had been a highlight for her parents. Family had been important to them. And now it fell to Noemi to pull her brothers together—she just wondered if that was even possible.

And what were they going to say when she revealed her news? Leo, well, she didn't think that he would feel one way or the other as they were still getting to know each other.

But Sebastian, he was a different story. Not so

long ago she thought she knew how he'd react, but over the past year he had grown rather distant and then with their parents' deaths, he just wasn't acting like himself.

Max approached her. He placed his finger beneath her chin, lifting her head until their gazes met. "What's the matter?"

"Why does something have to be the matter?"

He lowered his hand. "Because I know you. And you're worried. Are you afraid your brothers won't take the news of the baby well?"

She continued to stare into Max's eyes, finding strength in his gaze. "Sebastian and I haven't been getting along very well lately. I just… I don't know how he's going to take the news."

"Would it be easier if I wasn't here? You know, so you could talk to your brothers one-on-one."

She reached for his hand and squeezed it firmly. "I want you right here next to me." And then a thought came to her. "Unless you don't want to be here."

This time he squeezed her hand. "There's no place I'd rather be."

It was only then that she realized she'd been

holding her breath, awaiting his answer. "Have I told you lately how much I love you?"

"Mm…it has been a while. Almost a half hour."

She grinned at him. "How could I be so remiss?"

"I was worried you might have grown bored of me."

"That will never happen." She lifted up on her tiptoes and said in a soft, sultry voice, "I'll show you how much I love you later."

"Can't wait."

She pressed her lips to his. Her heart picked up its pace. There was no way that she'd ever grow bored of him. He was her best friend and her lover. He was her first thought in the morning and her last thought at night. If someone had told her that she could be this happy, she never would have believed them.

Someone cleared their throat.

Noemi reluctantly pulled away. Max smiled at her, letting her know that this would all work out. She ran her finger around her lips, drew in a deep breath and turned.

Sebastian's dark gaze met hers. She couldn't read his thoughts. She supposed she should have given him a bit of a heads-up about Max.

"Sebastian, thanks for coming. I'd like you to

meet Max." She'd intentionally left out the part about Max being a crown prince. She didn't want to overwhelm her brother all at once.

After the men shook hands, Noemi realized that he was alone. "Where are Maria and Frankie?"

"I… I don't think they're going to make it."

Before she could delve further into Maria's absence, the doorbell rang. That must be Leo. She would have to make sure to tell him that this was his home as much as theirs and there was no need for him to ring the doorbell.

She rushed to the door and swung it open to find that her brother wasn't alone. Standing next to him was a beautiful blonde with a warm smile.

"Come in." She glanced at Leo. "You know you don't have to ring the doorbell. This is your home, too. I hope that one day it will feel like it."

"Um…thank you." Leo's gaze moved to Sebastian and the smile faded from his face.

Not ready to deal with the tension between her brothers, she helped them with their coats and then walked them into the great room. Noemi turned to the woman with Leo and held out her hand. "Hi. I'm Noemi. Leo's sister."

"Nice to meet you. I'm Anissa. Leo's, um, friend."

"Girlfriend," Leo corrected, placing his arm around her slender waist.

"Welcome. I hope we'll get to be really good friends."

Just then the doorbell rang again. Noemi cast a glance over her shoulder at Sebastian. He moved toward the door and Noemi turned back to the get-to-know-you conversation going on between Leo and Max.

A few seconds later, she glanced back at the front door to see Maria and Frankie had arrived. Noemi smiled as she'd missed Maria and her nephew dearly. But seeing as Sebastian and Maria were having a hushed conversation, she didn't want to intrude. She really hoped those two would be able to patch things up.

A couple of minutes later, Sebastian, Maria and little two-year-old Frankie joined them in the great room. Noemi couldn't hold back any longer. With a big smile pulling at her lips, she rushed over to them.

"Hi." She gave Maria a quick hug. Then she knelt down in front of Frankie. His eyes were big as he glanced around the large room at all the people he didn't know.

"Hey, Frankie," Noemi said, trying to gain

his attention. When his gaze met hers, she said, "Can I have a hug?"

Frankie sent his mother a questioning look.

"It's okay," Maria said.

That was all it took for Frankie to release his mother's hand and let Noemi draw his little body to her. "I'm so happy you're here. I've missed you tons."

He pulled back and returned to his mother's side.

Noemi straightened. Her gaze moved to Maria, noticing the worry reflected in her eyes. "That goes for you, too."

Maria glanced in Max's direction. "I take it things are going well with you."

Noemi couldn't hold back an enormous smile. "Better than I could ever imagine."

"I'm so happy for you." The smile on Maria's lips didn't reach her eyes.

Noemi moved back to stand next to Max. He placed his arm over her shoulders. And then he leaned close. "Are you sure you want to do this now?"

She smiled up at him. He knew how nervous she was about her brothers' reactions—most especially Sebastian's. She nodded at him.

"Noemi," Sebastian said, "why did you call

us all here? Is it the attorney? Does he have news for us?"

She shook her head. "This isn't about the will."

"Then what is it about?" Sebastian's gaze moved to Max and then back at her. "You know I don't like guessing games."

Maria elbowed him and he quieted down. But it was her brother's stormy look that he gave his wife that worried Noemi. Instead of things getting better for these two, they appeared to be getting worse. Maybe when her brother heard her good news, he'd relax some, knowing that she wouldn't be bothering him about the business any longer. She clung to that hope as her brother hadn't been himself in a while.

"Maybe we shouldn't be here," Leo said, meaning him and Anissa.

"Of course you should," Noemi said. "You are my brother as much as Sebastian is. Our separation as kids was a horrible mistake, but I hope going forward that there will be no distance. Because I'm going to need all of you." When her brothers got worried looks on their faces, she said, "It's nothing bad. I promise. I… I'm pregnant. You're going to be uncles." And then glancing at the women, she added, "And aunts."

For a moment, there was silence as everyone took in the news.

Noemi's heart pounded. "And we're having twins."

Sebastian was the first to approach her. He had a serious look on his face and she wasn't sure what he was going to say.

"Are you happy?" he asked, in the same manner that their father would have asked.

She smiled at him. "I've never been happier."

He studied her face for a moment as though to make sure she was telling him the truth. And then he put his hands on her shoulders. "Then I am happy for you, too. Congratulations."

He pulled her into his arms and gave her a tight hug—something he hadn't done since they learned of their parents' deaths. She was so thankful that this time it was good news that had brought them together.

When Sebastian released her and backed away, Leo stepped up to her. "You do know that I have no idea about children or how to be a cool uncle, right?"

She smiled and nodded. "I think you'll figure it out. In fact, I'll insist." She reached out and hugged him. At first, he didn't move. His body was stiff and she thought that he was going to resist, but then he hugged her back.

When they pulled apart, Noemi moved to Max's side. She placed her hand in his, lacing her fingers with his. "Do you want to tell the rest?"

"You're doing fine."

Just the fact that he was standing there with her filled her with such happiness. All she needed was this right here—the people she loved. She needed to pinch herself to make sure this was all real, but she resisted the temptation.

"First, I should probably introduce Max by his proper name. I'd like you to meet Crown Prince Maximilian Steiner-Wolf. He is the heir to the throne of the European principality of Ostania."

Everyone's face filled with surprise. It felt so strange introducing him as a prince, as he was just Max to her. She really hoped his title and position wouldn't make a difference to her family.

Noemi drew in a deep breath and then slowly expelled it. "And he has asked me to marry him."

Maria said, "You'll be a princess."

"Wow," Anissa said in awe.

"Yes, she will," Max spoke up. "She will be the most beautiful and compassionate princess.

And I couldn't be luckier. I promise you that I will do my best to make her happy."

Sebastian's gaze moved between her and Max. "So you're moving to Ostania?"

Noemi nodded.

Max spoke up again. "I'm afraid that my duties are increasing and after Christmas, I will need to spend the bulk of my time in Ostania. I'm sorry to take your sister away from you all, but you will always be welcome at our home."

"Don't you mean your palace?" Maria asked.

Max nodded. "Yes. And trust me when I say it has a lot of guest rooms."

"Guest rooms that I expect all of you to use regularly," Noemi said. "Wait until you see this place. It's so beautiful. And they have great skiing. But I wanted you all to know that we will be here for Christmas. It'll be a family Christmas just like Mama and Papa would have wanted."

It would take time, but slowly they were coming closer together—just as their parents always wanted.

EPILOGUE

Five months later
Ostania Palace

"IT'S A BOY."

Max exited his wife's birthing chamber to carry his newborn son to the library, where the king, queen and his brother waited. He couldn't stop smiling. He'd never been happier.

Everyone oohed and aahed over Prince Leonardo Sebastian, named after Noemi's brothers. And after the decreed paternity test had been done a month ago, his son was now third in line for the throne. And when his sibling was born, they would be fourth in line.

"He's absolutely perfect," the queen declared with a big smile. And, to Max's surprise, she began to speak in baby talk to his son. His mother really did surprise him at times.

His father was doing much better after his transplant surgery. In the end, Tobias had been a perfect match and had given their father one of his kidneys. Both had come through the surgeries with flying colors.

"How's Noemi?" the queen asked.

"She's exhausted and resting before baby number two arrives. She came through Seb's delivery like a real trouper."

"Your Majesty?" came a voice from the doorway.

Every head in the room turned.

"Yes?" the king said.

The nurse looked a bit flustered. "I need Prince Max." She turned to Max. "The next baby is about to make its entrance into the world."

Max felt torn. His son was still in the queen's arms and she didn't look as though she planned to give him up any time soon.

"Go," the queen said. "I need a little time to get acquainted with my grandson." And then she turned back to the baby. "Your father acts like I've never been around a baby before."

Max didn't have time to argue with his mother. The baby should go back to the medical staff to be cared for before being passed around the room. Max turned to the nurse. "Will you take my son to the nursery?"

The older nurse smiled at him. "It would be my honor."

That's all Max needed to hear before he tore off down the hallway. He couldn't believe his blessing. Not that many years ago, he'd wondered if he'd live or die. And now he had the most loving wife and instead of being sterile, he'd fathered twins. It just proved that you never knew what was right around the next corner. You could never give up believing that there was something better—something amazing awaiting you if you just kept looking.

Max entered the chamber to find his wife groaning. He rushed to her side, taking her hand in his. He wished she didn't have to go through the pain. It didn't seem fair. But she didn't complain. She didn't yell at him like he'd read in some pregnancy blogs.

"You're doing amazingly," he whispered in her ear. "I love you." And then he kissed the top of her head.

In just a couple of minutes, the room filled with the loud cry of a baby.

The doctor held up the baby and smiled. "Your prince has a very healthy set of lungs."

"Yes, he does." Max smiled as his vision blurred with tears of joy. And then he turned back to his wife, who also had happy tears in her eyes. "You make beautiful babies."

"We make beautiful babies," she corrected.

"Yes, we do." He leaned down and kissed her lips.

Once again, Max cut the umbilical cord. The baby was cleaned up, wrapped in a blue blanket and handed over to his mother. Prince Alexandre, named after his grandfather, grew quiet as he gazed up at his parents.

Max's heart grew two times larger that day. He didn't know it was possible to love this much, but Noemi showed him each day that miracles really did come true.

* * * * *